MONTY SPLAIN

HORSE
Country

ISBN 978-1-66789-483-6 eBook 978-1-66789-484-3

CHAPTER 1

The first thing I remember in life is where horses come from.

I was only big enough to see through the gate boards in the barn and I saw that little horse come out of that big horse. My dad and two other men were helping.

I was thrilled. The little horse was cute and before long it was standing. The colt was shaky and wet. My dad wiped it off with grain sacks. Then he helped it feed on the mare, its mother.

I didn't think human babies could walk the same day as they were born, but there he was jumping around and eating. He must have been hungry because that's all he wanted to do.

I was in love with horses every day after that, my mother said. That was all I could talk about was the new little horse. I ran to the barn to check on him all the time.

My dad would ride the mare, that was his saddle horse, so I would take care of and play with the colt while he was gone.

One day, while my dad was gone on the mare, I got the bright idea that I should try to ride the colt. I was little and he was little, so I reasoned that it should work fine.

I got some hay and placed it by the fence so the colt would have to be near the fence to eat it. I climbed the fence and put out one leg over the colt's back, hanging onto the post with my hand to balance myself. When I was directly over his back I let go.

The colt was faster than I thought. He jumped out from under me and I ended up face first in the mud.

Wow, it seemed so easy for my father. He just put on the saddle and climbed on. That must be it. A saddle is what I needed. We only had one and it was too big for the colt. So that night I asked my dad for a small saddle. He smiled. I could tell he knew what I was up to, so he asked me what for, as if he didn't know.

"I want to ride the colt and go with you out to the pasture."

"Well, is the colt broke for riding?"

I was confused, "Broke?"

"Yeah," he said, "all animals must be trained, broke to ride, or pull a load with a harness or whatever you want them to do. Besides, the colt is only a yearling and it is too small to ride."

"When will he be old enough to ride?" I asked.

Dad said he really hadn't planned to break or train the colt, but just break it to sell.

"To sell," I said, "but what am I going to ride?"

Dad was surprised, "I didn't know you wanted to ride."

"I could go with you and help with the fence and the cows if I had a horse."

"I didn't start helping my dad until I was eight," he said. "You got a few years to go but you're about as big as I was then, so maybe I could use the help. I'm sorry son but I already traded this colt for some pure-bred Herefords, so we can upgrade our cattle herd."

"Upgrade, purebred, what are you talking about?"

"Well, you know our dogs are mutts. They came from many different breeds. All animals have different breeds, cows, horses, pigs, all of them. But the purer the breed, the higher the quality of the animal. That's why I want purebred Herefords. They are worth more for sale. In fact, out here you can't buy them. The only reason I could get these is because the owner wants this colt and agreed to a trade."

"Okay, I understand," I said.

"Tell you what, you can come ride with me and I'll show you how to ride the fence and fix it, so you can take over that job some day when you're ready to ride."

I couldn't wait.

CHAPTER 2

We traded the colt and got the purebred Herefords. They were good looking cows, I had to admit.

We were homesteaded way out west in Dakota Territory. My dad and mother were from over by Minnesota, but came way out west to homestead, almost to a place called Montana. Dad said all the good homesteads were taken back east and his brothers told him to homestead near the trail because that's the most likely place for the railroad to come through.

"Your property will be worth more there," they said.

A small village was starting up a few miles away and every year a few more homesteaders moved in, but we were still at the end of the line.

I started riding the fence and digging in the spring by my seventh birthday. My older brother, Barney, was much bigger than me so he had to run the team with the harrow. The team horses were much bigger than the saddle horse, but we never rode them. They pulled the wagon with all of us riding in the box to town or wherever we might be going.

I had a younger sister, Netty, and a younger brother, Carl, who were too small to help with anything except picking the eggs. Barney and I were always cranking the grain grinder, the cream separator, and pumping the butter churn. But by far, my favorite thing to do was to get on that horse and ride.

One day Harvey, a neighbor, stopped by to see if my dad would help with his horse who was having difficulty with a colt. When we got there Harvey and another man were examining the mare.

The other man had his arm all the way in there to try to see what was wrong. He looked very concerned and said, "the colt's foreleg was backwards and wrapped around its back."

I could tell from the look on their faces that this was not good. After some discussion it was decided to tie a rope to the colt to pull it out and try to save the mare. There was no mention of saving the colt.

I got a sick feeling in my stomach. We had lost some calves before and a lot of the time some of the pigs were born dead, but this was a colt.

Harvey and the helper got the rope around the colt and it was all that the three men could do to pull the colt out.

To our surprise, the colt was alive, and the mare lived through it too. Harvey said the mare had had several colts and was tough by now.

The colt's left foreleg was straight back. The helper pulled on it, but it had grown back. I didn't know what was going to happen, but I didn't have a good feeling about it.

Harvey said, "Well, the mare would probably reject it anyway."

I had a terrible feeling of what was about to happen. The little colt tried to get up, just like our colt had, but with only three legs I could tell she wasn't going to make it. My dad could see how I felt and tried to reassure me that it was for the best and that this happens.

"You know we lost calves and pigs before and horses are no different."

I yelled, "Can't we do something?"

The colt was beautiful in all aspects except for the out of place leg. We all stood there silently thinking about our problem. I could tell none of them wanted to destroy such a beautiful animal either.

"I'll take her," I finally said. "I'll figure some way to feed her and straighten her leg."

The helper said that colts don't have collar bones, only muscles and tendons that hold the forelegs to the shoulder blade, which has grown to this awkward shape. Straightening a leg like that has been done before but the leg will never have full strength. But with good hind quarters, the mare colt could be bred and do light draft work, which is mostly powered by the hind legs.

"Yeah," my dad said.

"So, I'll take her," I said. "Let me try."

Harvey looked at Dad and said, "Up to you Nels. The boy can have her if you want."

Dad looked at me and said, "It'll be a lot of work and you're not that big yet."

"I turn those cranks all the time. I'm stronger that you think."

"Well, the boy might learn a valuable lesson," Harvey said. "He's yours."

The pride welled up in me. I was a horse owner. Although it was what it was, I had my first horse.

Just then the mare got up and started to sniff and lick the colt.

"No rejection there," Dad said. "Maybe you don't want to give her away now."

"No," Harvey said, "I don't have time for it. Besides, I already gave her away and I don't go back on my word. You know, I don't need that mare for a few months so you could take her and milk her for the colt."

"I'll do it," I said. "Come on Dad, we need to get the wagon to haul her home."

I got the saddle and made Dad ride behind me. I ran the saddle horse all the way home.

I yelled at Barney to get the oxen. I needed the team of horses for the wagon.

"Why don't you use the oxen?" he asked.

"Too slow," I said as I unhitched the team of horses.

I ran them over to the wagon and heehawed them back into it. They knew what they were supposed to do. My mom and sister were watching all of this.

"It's time to eat," Dad said.

"We'll eat when we get back," I said.

Dad shrugged his shoulders at Mom, Netty, and Barney as we raced out of the yard.

"I got a horse," I yelled back at them trying to justify all the commotion.

It took all three of us to load the colt. We bridled the mare, and I rode in back to lead her, but the mare followed right along attentive to the colt.

"Drive careful," I yelled at Dad.

"Oh, drive careful now," he said. "Okay."

All three of them were still standing there wanting to see what we had.

"Wow," Barney said. "How did you get that horse? You don't have any money."

"Not the mare," I said, "this one." I pointed at the wagon.

"Oh, she's beautiful," Netty said hugging the colt's head, not noticing the leg.

Barney noticed right away and said, "Now I know how you got her. Do you think you can straighten it?"

"I'm going to try."

Dad said, "We better try to milk the mare. That colt has to be hungry."

Barney lifted the colt and carried him into the barn. I led the mare. Mom gave me a clean pail and to Dad's surprise the mare let him milk her. I think she knew it was for her colt. We had a lamb bottle, and the colt drank it all.

CHAPTER 3

The next day I milked the mare. Netty, now in love with the colt, fed her. We put hay in the loft with the block and tackle. I tried to lift the colt to drink but she was too heavy. I tried to balance her leg on the milk stool. When she tried to get her head under the mare the stool fell over, so I continued to milk. But the block and tackle gave me an idea.

When we were done with the hay, I got the block and tackle down and hooked it on a nail in the ceiling above the mare, but the nail fell out. The block and tackle were too heavy. So I carved one out of some smaller pieces of wood and some other lighter rope. I got a bigger nail and Dad helped me pound it all the way in.

I hooked the block to it and wrapped a grain sack around the colt's body and tied it to the block and tackle. Pulling the rope, the colt came off the floor. She put three legs down and tried to walk but was held by the grain sack. I then led the mare over to the colt. She could now bend down and feed without falling over. I fed the mare well and amazingly she knew to go to the colt to feed it.

Two days later, I was going to let the colt down for the night but to my surprise, she stood there on three legs, looking proudly at us. Netty, with tears, hugged the colt. Netty named the colt Lucky.

She said, "You are going to make it."

I also noticed that the leg was hanging down, so I pushed down on it and it was not as straight back as it had been.

The colt was getting stronger and could hobble around and eventually hobbled around to its mother and fed.

Dad was amazed at the progress. He knelt by Lucky and pushed the leg almost all the way down. Lucky whinnied loudly.

"It hurt," I said.

"Those muscles and tendons have to be stretched back into place and I think they will if we keep working at it. I don't think we'll ever get to ride her, but she will do a light draft and breed," he said.

Harvey showed up one day and said he would need his mare back soon.

Dad said, "Yeah, we will start weaning the colt."

I showed Harvey how the bad leg could reach all the way down to the ground.

"You have done a fine job," he said. "I'm glad the colt could be put to some use."

"Lucky is her name," I said.

"A good name for her," he replied.

We had Harvey in for supper of Mom's creamed fried chicken and corn on the cob. Harvey said his neighbor to the northeast had an older mare that couldn't pull with the team anymore but was still a rider and could also breed.

Harvey said he wanted to know if Dad wanted it. Dad told him he didn't need it.

Harvey said, "But your boy might."

"Yes," I almost yelled.

Silence.

I looked at Dad. He looked at Mom, and Mom looked at me.

"Not tonight," she said, "tomorrow."

"Okay, I promise," I said looking at Harvey who had a grin from ear to ear.

"I remember my first horse too," he said.

"Thanks."

"Well, you did a good job with that colt. She should not have made it."

"Lucky," Netty said.

CHAPTER 4

I was turning the churn crank so fast to finish my chores, it was squeaking. Mom barely got the pancakes made, adding molasses and chokecherry syrup, and I was gone.

We galloped around the fence and the spring was still open. I then turned northeast to Harvey's neighbor. Dad's saddle horse was no spring chicken, but I got her to trot all the way there.

Ben was one of the first homesteaders in this county. His horses had aged, but he bought several new ones back east and had nothing to do with his older ones.

"Wow, how many do you have?" I asked.

"Two now, but one is a gelding, and nobody would want him. No breeding there," he said.

"I'd look at him," I said.

Ben told me where to find them and said to bring them back into their yard, so I did. There were four of them.

Ben pointed to the two he didn't need. I was surprised they didn't look bad, but Ben said they were past their prime and he would never use them again.

"What are you going to do with that gelding?" he asked.

"I want to breed the mares and ride the gelding in the meantime."

"My brother lives east of Colgan and I think he might have some old horses too," he said. "I don't know what they are, but you could ride there and check them."

His wife made coffee and pie. Their children had grown and left, so they wanted to visit. I was antsy to get home with my new horses, but for free horses I could visit for a while.

We talked about the new church, meeting house, and school room we built in the community. It was good I guess, but now I was going to have to go to school.

Mom taught us letters and arithmetic and I figured I knew it all. Enough anyway.

I finally excused myself and promised to return to visit.

I saddled the gelding and was surprised at his go. But by the time I got home, he showed his age. He was still a rider with just not as much endurance as a younger horse. He would probably tire fast pulling a draft.

Dad and Barney came out when they saw the three horses coming in.

Barney said, "How do you do it? You go to get one horse and come back with two."

I told them the whole story including that I might have a lead on two more.

Mom called "supper", so we put up the horses and went in.

"What are you going to do with this old gelding?" Barney asked.

"Ride the fence with him while the mares are at Uncle Ed's getting bred."

They looked at each other.

"Does that mean my horse is going to get bred too?" Dad asked.

"Why not?" I asked.

"You're going to have a whole herd."

"Yes," I said. "I will finish fencing the half section, build more corrals, break more land, and mow more hay."

Carl asked, "What are you going to do with all of the horses?"

"Breed them and sell them," I said.

Mom asked if I was going to have time to go to the new school.

"You taught me to read, add, subtract, and my writing is pretty good."

Mom looked at me and said, "There's a lot more to learn."

"But what?"

Dad sat me down at the kitchen table. Barney, Netty, and Carl were listening.

"Son, you can go around here, local and buy and sell. Everybody knows everybody else. They know you're not a thief. But if you get far away, people won't know if you stole those horses. That's why they are branded with a registered brand. The brand inspector can verify they are your livestock."

"But how do you prove their yours if you buy stock with somebody else's brand?" I asked.

"Well, that's where a bill of sale comes in. You will need to read it, write it, and understand what it is. Of course, you will need to be able to add and subtract to know how much you are paying or receiving for your stock. It must all be there on the bill of sale."

"Now I know this is old horse stock you got, and they probably won't go anywhere else. But if you buy anything somewhere else, especially if it is branded, you better have some paperwork to prove they are yours."

"This all used to be outlaw country until the homesteaders came in here and tamed it. But just west over in Montana, there is still outlaw country, lots of rustlers and thieves. Land, no law. A few brave souls have ventured to ranch over there, but they live by the gun."

"I don't know when law and order will come to that country, but for now you could get into real dangerous trouble if you don't have a legitimate claim in whatever you're in possession of. There's so little law over there those citizens have formed vigilante groups to track down outlaws and rustlers. They hanged several of them without a trial."

"What's a rustler?" Carl asked.

"A man that steals somebody else's cows," Barney said.

"Yeah," Dad said. "They have open range over there, so they have to leave their stock out unprotected. The herd is hard to watch all the time so there's easy picking for rustlers.

We have way fewer stock here so we can keep an eye on them. That's why you ride the fence every day. We know our neighbors and have better law enforcement, so that's why we have to have better quality stock, so they are worth more per head."

"I see," I said.

"So you better learn how to write out a bill of sale."

Mom and Dad sat down, and we wrote out several bills of sale to practice. My father then went to his hiding place and showed us the bill of sale for the trade of the pony for the pure-bred registered Herford cattle he got. It had the brands and was signed by both parties involved.

"Wow, what if some rustlers stole a bunch of cows, got away with them, wrote a bill of sale, and signed somebody's name to it?"

"That could be a problem," Dad said, "but so far most of the rustlers are too dumb to know how to write."

"Okay," I said. "I get the point."

CHAPTER 5

I worked hard that summer; built fence, plowed, and hayed extra for the upkeep of my extra horses. I had seven now and was hoping that four of them were bred.

My little Lucky wouldn't be bred until next year. She had grown amazingly. She followed me everywhere like a dog. She ate everything, even the top of the carrots in Mom's garden. I thought I was in trouble, but Mom said to dig them up. They were big enough. But as I dug them, there behind me was Lucky eating the carrots, too. Horses eat anything. I had to put her in the corral with the other horses and she didn't like it.

She hardly limped at all now, but still didn't have the strength to carry a man and saddle. I would breed her next year.

We had a good year. We got lots of fencing done, lots of hay put up, and then came the grain harvest. We had a thrashing gin, hand cranked of course.

Barney and I cranked all day. Dad threw the wheat in the air on windy days to separate the chaff. He could throw high with the scoop. Most of the chaff blew away and the wheat fell into the wagon. Then the chickens scratched through and ate the chaff.

With Barney and I helping, we had the most productive year on Dad's homestead. We finally finished most of the hard work. I was still riding the fence of the north pasture and digging the spring.

The gelding seemed to strengthen with good feed and exercise. I would ride him north, exploring upwards toward Canada, the other country. Montana was another state, but Canada was, I was told, a whole different country with different laws and government. I didn't know what it meant to go there.

Ben said he rode there a couple of times but couldn't see anything. He said after trouble with the Indians, they were now starting to settle the place but he didn't know much more than that. I rode up a little further each day. You couldn't tell where it was. It all looked the same to me.

I strayed there a few miles when I suddenly saw two riders coming right at me. Wow, was I in trouble? Nobody warned me about going up there, but these guys were bearing down on me fast. I knew the gelding was already tired, so I waited. They both had rifles on the side of their saddles and as they got closer, I also saw revolvers in their belts.

I froze, not knowing what to do. These guys, like what I had been told, were cowboys.

They rode up and in a funny voice said, "Howdy."

I said, "Howdy."

They asked where I was from and I said south of here.

"Oh, down at the states," one of them said. They had me.

"Yeah," I said. "Am I not in the states now? I'm just here looking for a lost horse."

They both perked up and said, "We don't know. There are no markers around here. But speaking of horses, we came down to buy some of them. Would you have any for sale?"

Wow, I thought, my excuse worked. They don't seem to mind that I am here at all and even want to buy some horses.

Not thinking what to say and wanting to get home I said, "Well, I don't know of any. But if you follow me to the farm, my dad might know of some."

"Okay, my name is Arvine and this is Tex." They both laughed. "We wish we were Texans but we are Canadians."

"My name is actually Sem, short for a long funny name but Sem will do."

We shook. I was relieved. They didn't know where the line was either.

As we rode to the farm, I asked them about Canada. They were just getting settled there. They were going to have homesteading like the states.

I asked if they ranched.

"Only horses," they said. "We get horses, train them, and sell them to the settlers coming out. Most of the wild horses in Canada have been caught and now the only other place to get them was in the states."

Right away I thought of the outlaw trail in Montana and it led to Canada. It suddenly made sense where the ill-gotten livestock were going. I wasn't so comfortable anymore.

My dad and Barney were out in the field, so I took them there, away from the house, even though they seemed very friendly.

Dad told them he didn't know of any right off hand, but after thinking about it for a minute, he then asked them what kind of money they had. Arvine pulled out some paper and said it was Canadian script.

Dad examined it and asked if we could have the bankers in town look at it. Wow, why would Dad want to do that? I could tell Barney was surprised too.

"Sure thing, we can take it there now if you want."

"Okay. Barney, finish up here. Bill, saddle my horse."

While I saddled Dad's horse, he continued to talk to the Canadians. We set out for town. Dad told them to follow.

When we were ahead of them Dad said in a low voice, "They are paying good money if this script is good. I think we should sell."

I almost fell off my horse. "We sell."

"I haven't told you, but my horses are getting old and my dad in Minnesota is looking for a new team and saddle horses for us and you know what happens to old horses around here."

This was so sudden.

He said, "I think we can buy one or two more younger horses for what they pay us for these."

Wow, what a shock. My head was spinning what to do.

We got into the bank and the head man whom Dad knew well said that the script would have to be sent to Crosby for verification.

"Three days," he said.

To my surprise Arvine and Sem agreed to that.

"So, three days from now me and Sem will be back. We can dicker then."

"Okay," Dad said.

They shook both of our hands. I, the boy, they didn't leave me out. They shook my hand too. I felt important.

As we rode away, I said, "Wow Dad, I'm surprised they just left their money there like that."

"Well, I don't think they could buy any horses if they didn't prove up their money. Son, listen. For what they said they would pay, anybody around here would sell because we can pick up younger, better stock in Minnesota for less money. I heard Canada was desperate for horse stock. Where did you find them anyway?"

Caught, I admitted that I rode way up north just to explore and ran across them. I was scared at first, seeing those guns, but they didn't know where the border was either.

"Well, I should be mad at you, but you may have found us a deal."

CHAPTER 6

"My dad gave me that team as a wedding present. They were his old ones. My saddle horse is at least 20 years old. The only one of yours that's young is the colt."

Wow, did I have some thinking to do.

Dad added, "As well, you know those foals don't always turn out."

"Yeah," and I didn't even know how many of them were even bred. The more I thought about it the more I thought Dad was right. My horses had become my pets, but I would have to part with them sooner rather than later. I really wanted at least a really good saddle horse.

I talked myself into selling by the third day. By noon, we decided to ride to town. If Sem and Arvine didn't show, we could at least find out if the script was any good.

My heart was pounding. No sign of the Canadians. Now that I had set my mind to sell, I supposed the deal would fall through.

The banker waved us into his office, the first time I had been in there.

"Sit down," he said with a grim look on his face. "Yes, we can convert it 18 to 1."

I looked at Dad.

"Okay," he said. "We've got good money now if they show up."

"They have to," I said. "They wouldn't just leave their good money here, would they?"

"No," the banker said. "I think they'll be here."

We left and after picking up some things, went back to the farm.

"Dad," I said, "if we sell, we won't have any horses."

"We'll ride the train to Minnesota as soon as we can and pick up the new horses," Dad said.

Sem and Arvine were at the farm when we got there.

"Let me talk, Bill. Just listen."

We shook. After some small talk Sem and Arvine went to inspecting the horses. They knew horses and after a thorough inspection, we started the money offers. Dad added that the mares should be bred.

When they started to inspect the yearling, I said, "It's not for sale because it has a bad leg." I pointed it out and told of the birthing problems, but they still seemed to be interested in the horse.

"Five hundred dollars for the team, one hundred dollars per horse, one hundred fifty dollars for the bred mares," they said.

I could tell Dad was interested but insisted on six hundred dollars for the team and they agreed, so he would get seven hundred fifty dollars for his three horses.

They still wanted all seven of mine and offered nine hundred dollars for all.

I told them I wanted to keep the colt as it was partially lame anyway.

"Nine hundred fifty dollars for all," Arvine returned.

Nine hundred fifty dollars was a lot of money. I looked at Dad.

He took me aside and said, "We will go to Minnesota as soon as we can. Go for it."

I told Arvine okay, and we shook on it.

We headed back to the bank in Colgen. At the exchange rate of 18 to 1, they were a little short of the total amount needed, so we agreed to keep the colt until they could get back with the rest of the script.

They were set to head back to Canada when I remembered the bill of sale. So we went to the house and Dad had me make mine out, names, dates, brands, horse markings, and price. Mine was very similar to Dad's. We all signed. After coffee and pie they were on their way.

"So my bill of sale was okay?" I announced proudly to Dad.

"All except your penmanship," Mom replied.

"Penmanship?" I said, confused.

"Yeah," Netty said. "We can't read your writing."

"We'll help you with that," Mom said.

"Well son, you now have more money than this whole farm makes in an entire year."

"Yeah, and at least you didn't have to sell Lucky," Netty said.

"Well," Barney said, "they are coming back for him."

Netty wasn't happy but Mom consoled her with it being like puppies, the next one will be better than the last.

We were sitting there, proud of ourselves.

Dad said he was surprised they were not really concerned about the bill of sale.

"Yeah," I said. "I guess the laws in Canada are different."

"You mean like possession is nine-tenths of the law?" Barney asked.

"No, Canada would have to have some sort of livestock marking and ownership system. I know they have brands up there," Dad added.

"Dad, when's the next train to Minnesota? I'll be ready tomorrow. We are on foot on this farm."

"No," Barney said. "We have the oxen to pull the wagon."

We had more money than we ever had, but I felt empty. Somehow, the horse represented freedom and adventure to me. We were somehow restricted to the farm. I was desperate. I even tried putting the saddle on Lucky. But after trying to put my weight on her I gave that up. I wondered if Sem and Arvine would be back for her.

On Sunday, we hitched the oxen to the wagon. We all laughed, off to Church we went at two miles per hour.

Netty said, "Come on Barney, can't we go faster? I can walk faster than this."

It was only four and a half miles to Church and we better make it on time.

People stared at us. One neighbor asked if all our horses ran away. I decided I didn't want to be without a horse again.

Arvine and Sem were back within a week. We exchanged the script for Lucky and again they didn't insist on a bill of sale.

Netty helped me with my penmanship and I was proud of the bill of sale. I had practiced. Sem and Arvine asked when we would have some more horses for sale.

"How many do you need?" I asked.

"We seem to sell all we can get. The settlers are coming west and they need horses, so maybe all you can get."

They were off to pick up some other horses they bought.

CHAPTER 7

I was after Dad every day now to go to Minnesota. We needed horses badly. The oxen were slow and only worked eight hours a day, but they could do a lot of work only eating hay. Horses needed grain but were faster and worked as long as you did. We had a lot of work to do. I was tired of walking the fence and carrying the fence plyers and staples. I didn't carry my .22 rifle anymore, too heavy with everything else. The gophers were devastating our pastures.

Dad was just too busy to go, so I said, "I could go by myself. I'll take the train to Minnesota. Grandpa, Grandma, and Uncle Ned could help me load the horses on the train. Then it would be just a matter of riding the train back."

"Son, you're only 16. That's too young for such a job."

"But we'll never get all of our work done without horsepower."

That put dad into deep thought. He headed to the house and put the idea to Mom. She got a worried look on her face.

"Well, he's kind of right, honey. We are getting further behind with fall's work. As much as I would like to see my parents and brother, we could spare him for a few days to get the horses."

My mother knew she had to consider it, being as Dad had proposed it.

"Dad, we'll take a load of grain to Crosby and I'll catch the train then."

"We could load the wagon tonight," Barney said.

Dad looked at me and said, "Well, you have shown good sense and ability to this point. But you know you would be taking almost all our money with you. Do you understand the responsibility that would be?"

"Oh yes. Nobody on that train would have to know I have a dollar on me. I would tell everybody

I was going to visit my grandparents with no mention of business. So why would they think I would be carrying any money at all? Uncle Ned and Grandpa could handle all the yearlings and help me get on the train. Then it's just a ride home."

After supper, Barney, Dad, and I shoveled the wagon full of wheat. No use going to town without hauling some grain in.

Our wagon was a wooden box with two axels, and four wheels under it, and a hitch in front. It would haul fifty bushels of grain in it. It didn't have a seat, only a 2" x 6" plank across the top of the box to sit on. It had some weak spots, but the blacksmith in Colgan built iron supports and bolted them on to reinforce it.

The next morning Dad and I headed to Crosby with our wheat and one thousand eight hundred dollars of our horse money. We had plenty of time to talk with the slow plodding oxen. He again reminded me that there were a lot of dishonest people in the world and that we were isolated in our small corner of the world. He reiterated that I should only trust Uncle Ned and Grandpa.

Then he said something that shocked me. He was considering getting a team of mules.

"Wow, you mean those funny looking little horses with long ears?" I looked as disgusted as I could.

He said they were much cheaper than a big, matched team of draft horses and don't eat so much grain and hay.

"Grandpa has a set of young draft horses you are to bring back and I will need a saddle horse, a breeder preferably. I guess you can choose whatever horses you can find there. We did good with the Canadian sale, so maybe it would be a good investment to get better, breedable horse stock."

"And just for me, look at some mules and what a good team would cost. I know you're not excited about it, but I would like to try a set some day. Have Uncle Ned help you."

"Okay," I promised.

The train was already in Crosby, so I got a ticket and we checked on getting a stock car for returning with the horses. They said it would be no problem because stock cars were sent west all the time to return cattle east.

I was excited, my first train ride. As we pulled out of town some boys on horses tried to keep up with the train, but we quickly outdistanced them. I waved goodbye.

I had only seen my Grandparents, Uncle, and his wife once before. They brought some of our stuff out from Minnesota to our homestead, but that was awhile back. I was a lot smaller then. Mom and Dad wrote all the time. That's how we knew that they had horses for sale.

The train was exciting. We were moving a lot faster than I expected. We arrived in Grand Forks that evening. I slept in the station until my train south left in the morning.

A short ride south to the first stop. Then twenty some miles east across the river to near Crookston. I started walking but soon caught a ride with a delivery wagon. Everyone here was very friendly and helpful and soon I reached my grandparent's farm.

They were glad to see me. Uncle Ned and his wife had two children, a boy and girl, my cousins whom I had never met. It seemed like the talk would never end. This late in the fall, they had completed most of their summer crop work.

Every quarter section seemed to have a farm on it, so the neighbors were numerous. They all wanted to know about western Dakota. It was a never-ending job of trying to talk about it.

I was starting to get antsy to see the horses, but it was one picnic or gathering after another. Of course, I had to stay for Sunday church and meet more people.

My grandmother could see I was antsy to get going but made the point that after you come all the way out here, you need to stay and visit awhile. Seemed to me like that was about all they did around here.

I explained to them that we had a new church, but other than that, we were breaking raw, rough land and there wasn't time for much else.

I explained how we had been lucky and sold all our horses to the Canadians for a good price. Now we need to replenish our horse stock.

Grandpa had the draft team Dad wanted and the select saddle horse.

I told them that I was looking for brood mares and a stallion to start a herd.

My uncle was impressed, "At sixteen years of age you have ambition boy."

We found four good mares, but the only stallion we found at a neighbor's house was not for sale.

"Too dangerous," they said. They couldn't tame him.

I asked why they hadn't gelded him then.

"Can't catch him to even do that," they said.

So we went to look at him, all black and wild.

"I think he would kill a man if he could," the owner said. "If we can't do something with him, we'll have to do something about him."

"Speaking of wild, how is that west country, any horse thieves or rustlers out there? That area used to be lawless. Whole place was nothing but outlaws and Indians at one time I heard."

"Well, it's pretty civilized now," I said. "Lots of homesteaders and towns are popping up. I heard all of that moved on west into Montana. They call it the outlaw trail over there."

"Have you ever been there?" Uncle Ned asked.

"No," I said, "but I plan to as soon as I get a good saddle horse. Someday I'd like to go across that country. The train is going to cross it at some point. You know, when I rode the train here, it only took two days. You all should come over and see it."

I could tell they were all interested.

"Yeah, we have young ones that might have to come out there and homestead someday."

We finally got back to the stallion search, either not for sale or gelded. So, I told my uncle I planned to be back next year and that he should look for me a stud horse. He and Grandma promised they would.

I was finally off with seven horses, four saddles, and tack that I had bought. All were fine young animals that would bring a premium on the Canadian market. But I was of a mind to start a good line of horse business.

After tethering the horses together and getting some feed loaded across the other saddle, I was ready for the trip home. Grandma loaded me down with lots of grub for the road.

Uncle Ned and his son wanted to accompany me back to the station. We got as far as the river and the ferry. I told Ned that I could make it from there.

"No need for you to have to pay the ferry also."

He agreed and promised to find us some more good horse stock for the return trip next year.

CHAPTER 8

After crossing, I got to the station. The north train had already gone by for the day and there would not be a stock car for tomorrow's train. Wow, I hadn't anticipated this. I sat for a while contemplating my situation.

The station had a map of all the train tracks across the state. The east west track from Grand Forks to Crosby was not that far north from where I was, so I decided to ride northwest and intersect the track further west and ride it from there. I had Grandma's food with me, so I figured I could ride a long way before I would need to find food.

It turned out to be easy to find my way. The sun headed west and there's lots of section lines there. Also, the trails and roads were well established with almost every quarter section homesteaded.

I stopped at a farm that night to ask if I could stay in their barn for the night. Lars and his wife were an older couple. They were very nice and insisted I stay in their house. Their children were grown and gone, and the bedroom was empty.

I would have been more comfortable in the barn, but they insisted. After supper, we talked too late. Lars gave me some bad news. I was headed straight to the lake and I would have to go north or south from here to get around it if I wanted to continue west. Then he told me I should have a straight shot northwest from there. It sounded like the south route would be the shortest.

After breakfast I thanked them and tried to pay them, but they said no. They enjoyed the company too much.

I headed south and drifted west and sure enough a big lake and mud flat appeared off to the west.

Not too happy with myself for not asking for directions, I moved around the big lake. About four hours later, I was around and heading northwest again. Half a day lost but now I was on course again.

This was not like back home. There were numerous farms everywhere and most of the people were very friendly. I realized nobody asked for my paperwork to prove I owned the horses. I guess most people were considered honest here.

I came to a farm to stay. They had two horses for sale, one mare and one gelding. I told him I only needed the mare, but he knew how to bargain.

One hundred dollars for the mare or one hundred fifty dollars for both. The horses looked good. I don't know what I was thinking, but they were good sales for the Canadians. I ended up getting free room and board and two more horses. I now had eight trailing the one I was riding.

The farms became fewer and farther between, but I was still finding places to stay. The land turned sandier and the grass was not so good. I ran into a livestock operation. Sure enough, it had to happen, mules everywhere. Bruce Clemenson was a mule breeder. He invited me in, said his wife died and was welcome for the visit.

I got the big sales speech for mules. As we talked, he saddled one for a test ride. He could tell I was skeptical. What the hell, I jumped on. I was surprised, a strong hard running animal. By the time I was back, I admitted the potential was there.

As I looked them over, he said two hundred dollars a piece or three hundred dollars for a good working team. I should have known. Dad was right. Three hundred dollars compared to one thousand dollars for the draft horses was a good deal. I told him my father was the farmer and that I would let him know about your mules.

The next morning as I left, I had to admit I was impressed with the mules. But they sure were nothing to look at like a horse.

CHAPTER 9

I didn't know how far I was from the railroad, but I was getting a long way towards home. I'd ask at the next farm, but the further west I got, the fewer farms there were. Getting antsy to get home I rode till midnight. A big moon led us on.

We finally stopped at a stream with lots of good grass about. I hadn't seen a homestead light for the last ten miles or so. I guess I'd have to bed down right out here with the horses.

I'd never done this before, so I staked the horses to some small bushes by the stream and used the two half sacks of feed and the two saddles as a bed. The horses stayed amazingly close by. Maybe they didn't want to get too far from the feed.

They were all right there, laying around in the morning. I planned to stay at a farm and buy some food there, but it didn't work out and I was getting hungry. Two small jerky and a half a biscuit was all that was left in the saddle bags, so I was antsy to ride.

The horses didn't disappoint. We trotted most of the morning. I changed off horses to keep any one of them from getting too tired. I was traveling a good distance that way and before too long was back to signs of civilization.

Before I decided to stop, I came to a town. It was Crosby. I had paralleled the train track all the way home. Obviously, I had traveled more west than north.

After finding a good meal there, I decided I could make it to my Uncle's house by sun fall. They were excited to see me. Uncle Ed said my parents were watching for me and claimed I was overdue to return. At supper I explained everything to Uncle Ed, his wife, and kids and then got a good night's sleep in a bed.

I arrived back home shortly after noon. Mom was frantic to see me.

"What took so long?" she asked.

After a second explanation of the whole trip, I asked where Dad and Barney were.

"They're trying to keep the fence up at the north place."

I saddled two of the new mares and headed north. Dad and Barney were fixing fence with the oxen on the wagon. The cows were out. Dad yelled, grabbing one of the horses. He yelled back at Barney to get the fence mended. Dad explained to me that they had not been able to check the fence so often with me gone and no horses. The cattle got out and we were hot on their obvious trail.

"Wow," I said to Dad, "horse tracks."

Sure enough, at least two or three horse tracks among the cattle tracks.

"Did that fence fall down or was it pulled down?" I asked.

"Come to think of it, it could have been pulled down," he said. "Two posts down and broken wire, could have been."

"Wow, are we trailing rustlers?" I asked.

He looked at me with a concerned look and said, "We've never had a problem around here, but could be."

No guns with us but we pressed on anyway. I figured we were well into Canada when we crossed a ridge. There at the water hole were our cattle.

Dad grabbed my arm, "If these are rustlers, they might be dangerous."

"I know," I said.

What can we do? We couldn't see any riders down there, but they could be lurking about, letting the cattle rest while they checked out the area.

I spotted a long stick, about four feet long. I grabbed it and began whittling on it.

"Let's proceed down there," I said. "If somebody comes back, this stick, from a distance could look like a rifle. At least they wouldn't think we were unarmed."

"Yeah," Dad said. "Good idea. Let's go."

As we got closer, There were shoed horse tracks in the mix. But there were more, heavy deep tracks, either big horses or horses with riders. I studied the tracks, wondering if it could have been Sem and Arvine. I mentioned it to Dad.

"They always paid good money and seemed honest to me," Dad said.

"Yeah, I agree. I just brought it up because they knew where our cattle were and that I was gone."

"Yeah, good point," Dad said. "Can't think of anybody else that would have known that."

We got the cattle headed home after I checked to see if the other two sets of tracks had left the area and sure enough, the tracks headed straight north. I studied the tracks and made a mental note of exactly what they looked like, so I could check them against any other tracks I came across.

Dad asked, "What took you so long, over two weeks?"

I told him about all the visiting, horse trading, and what I brought home. Then I told him about the train situation and how I decided to trail the horses home.

"You trailed them?"

"Yeah."

"You could have run into all kinds of problems," he said.

"Other than going around the lake, it wasn't bad."

"Your mother won't like to hear that."

"I know. But Dad, I still have over $300 left. I didn't have to buy the train ticket."

"Wow," he smiled. "Good point. But still, we better stick to the safe way."

"Okay," I said. "Dad, it would be so easy for you and Mom to go back on the train to visit. Barney and I can handle everything here if you want to go."

Yeah, you could, he thought. "We just might do that."

We got the cattle back that night. It was dark but Barney had the fence fixed.

The next morning Mom was none too happy with me not taking the train home as I had promised. I tried to console her, saying she and Dad should take a trip back and visit her family. I pulled the three hundred dollars out of my pocket and said we easily have the money now that I hadn't bought a train ticket.

"Oh, you reckless boy," she said, kissing me on the cheek. "Will you never learn?"

I had to hear the story again of her reckless older brother that had taken off on a horse trip and never returned. Nobody ever found out what happened to him.

We didn't tell the rest of the family about the horse tracks that were in our cattle tracks. Dad got word to the sheriff and he met us at the north pasture. His deputy was with him. It was just Dad and I there. We told them the whole story.

"But you say they could have broken out and wandered also?"

"Yeah, that's what we figured at first, but there were different horse tracks in with them."

"Wow," he said, "we haven't had a real rustling case since I became sheriff. All wandered off or some other reason. If they were headed to Canada, that's where they'd take 'em. You are as far out here to the west as the homesteading has come so you are as close to the old outlaw trail as anybody. All I can say is you better keep a look out. We'll do some snooping around also."

I told him about my horses, my concern for rustling, and that I still needed a stud horse.

"There's going to be an auction for a stud horse down in Watford," the Deputy said.

"They caught and shot the Missouri Kid down there and they are auctioning off his big stud stallion to pay for his funeral. I hear he is a big, virile stallion."

"What is an auction?" I asked.

"Everybody that wants the horse will be there and they will all offer what they want to pay for the horse," the sheriff said, "and the highest bidder will get it."

"Wow, a real breeding stallion."

"Be there on the 14th by 1:00 and you can bid."

"Okay. Thanks."

We shook and they said to let them know if anything came up. They rode away.

"Dad, there's my chance. I need to get these mares and your saddle horse bred if I'm going to be in the horse business. I could even get some stud fees."

"Yeah, if the Canadians keep paying like they have, could be a good bet."

CHAPTER 10

Before the 14th came around, Arvine and Sem showed up on another horse buying expedition. They weren't having much luck and checked out our newest horse stock.

"Where'd you get 'em?" Sem asked.

I explained that our relatives acquired them in Minnesota, a long way away. As we talked, I maneuvered my way around so I could study their hoof prints. They noticed and asked if I was inspecting their horses.

"Well, I always like to look at good horse stock," I said. Luckily, their hoof prints didn't match what I had seen. "It took me a week to get these home. These are my new breeding stock. Hopefully, I will have more horses for sale for you someday."

"What about the gelding?" Arvine asked.

"I was going to use him when the mares were pregnant."

"We'll be back in a couple weeks."

"Okay," I said. "See you then."

That night at supper I told Dad that Arvine and Sem had been there. Their prints didn't match the ones we saw that day at the water hole.

"I'm glad to hear that," he said.

"What if they weren't riding the same horses?" Carl asked.

Dad and I looked at each other. The mystery wasn't over.

I was tending the north pasture and cattle everyday now. Dad admitted we were getting a lot more done with all the horsepower around.

Carl was riding now and would follow me up to the pasture. Unfortunately, he wasn't big enough to fix fence yet. Carl was able to shoot the .22, but still had some practicing to do to help with the gopher population. I told Carl he'd have to ride the fence by himself tomorrow. I was going to the horse auction.

I had six hundred dollars from my bank account and rode to Watford. There were a lot more people there than I figured should have been for only one horse. I figured five hundred dollars was enough for the horse but brought six hundred dollars just in case the horse was exceptional. It was a four to five year old black stallion, well trained and good temper.

To my surprise the bidding started at five hundred dollars. I only got one bid in at five hundred fifty dollars, but it soon went beyond that to seven hundred fifty dollars. Wow, it was going to be difficult to get a good stud horse.

I must have been looking dejected because the sheriff who conducted the sale came up to me and said that he still had the tack and guns for sale.

I answered back that I had come for the horse.

"Well, look at this," he said, "a big black saddle with silver inlay and a brand on the back corner."

It was something, but probably not practical for farm use. I was looking at the saddle bags and wondering what the Canadians would pay for this, when the sheriff brought out two nickel plated Colt 45 revolvers and a Winchester 44 - 40 lever action rifle. He could tell they caught my eye.

"Fifty dollars for the whole works."

"This isn't something I need," I told him.

"Well," he said, "you were bidding over five hundred dollars for that horse. Did you have that much money?"

"Yeah," I said, and pulled my cash out to show him.

I suddenly realized what I had done. Dad had said, don't ever show anybody you have money, not even the sheriff. Now that he knew I had money; he did the hard sell. I liked the big saddle bags. I opened them and they were empty.

"We kept all the ammo and stuff," the sheriff said. "We can use it, but we have no use for this."

I felt the 45s. Wow, they felt good and the Winchester was something I'd always wanted. Then I remembered we hadn't had a gun when we saw the hoof prints with the cattle and Dad was concerned about it. Nah, what a funny notion. I didn't need such a gun.

I asked him, "How much for just the saddle and tack?"

"All or none," he said. "I need to get rid of it all."

"Well Okay. Thanks anyway," I said turning to my horse.

"Forty dollars for all," he said. "That's a fifty dollar saddle brand new."

The Canadians bought every extra saddle we had, and I wondered if they had a shortage of guns up there too.

Why not, "thirty dollars," I said.

"Oh no, I'd buy them for thirty dollars myself for that."

"Thirty five dollars," I said.

"Thirty eight dollars, low as I can go."

I looked at the Winchester and grabbed my money, "Thirty eight dollars, paid in full. I need a bill of sale."

"For that," the sheriff said, "possession is nine-tenths of the law."

"Yeah," I said, "but that saddle has a brand on it."

"Okay, follow me to the office." He said with a sigh.

I realized I had two saddles and one horse, but I had money. I could buy a resale horse to carry the other saddle. The sheriff handed me the bill of sale and pointed me to the livery stable. Most livery stables have some old horses for sale, but not this one.

"Did you see what that stallion went for?" the smith asked.

"Yeah, I know," I said.

"You're in ranch country and horses are a high commodity around here."

Feeling the fool, with two saddles and one horse, I tried to mount the black saddle on the other one, but it didn't work. The old saddle did ride on the bigger black one. Off I went riding on two saddles and guns sticking out everywhere. People stared at me all the way to Williston.

I thought I'd try to buy another resale horse there if I could. It was late when the stable boy came out laughing.

"I've seen a lot of cowboys with two horses and one saddle, but never one horse and two saddles."

"Good laugh," I said. "You got any horses for sale?"

"I think we got one old pony for sale, but the bosses won't be back 'til morning."

"Okay, I'll sleep in the barn."

"Okay."

Morning came and I went to find something to eat. By the time I got back, the boss was there. He showed me the old pony.

"Fifty dollars."

"Okay," I said.

I was sure he was a good reseller for the Canadians.

CHAPTER 11

Carl was mowing hay when I got back. I suddenly realized I needed to do more because my horses would need hay and feed for the winter.

We worked long days breaking more ground and cutting hay. Dad had us take a few days off alternately to rest up. I wanted to do some exploring to the west anyway. So on my rest days, I took my best saddle horse and headed to Montana to see what the outlaw trail looked like.

The rolling hill country leveled off in places of flat staked plains. Soon I came to funny looking, large horned cattle with a Circle C brand grazing in the field. I eventually ran into a cowboy. Gus informed me that they would soon be rounding up the cattle to be driven to the rail head to be sold and that I could get a job helping with the roundup. I told him I really didn't need a job, but he insisted.

"Go see Harlen. We need all the help we can get."

Out of curiosity, I followed his directions to the cook wagon to find the foreman.

A herd of thirty some horses were being held around the cook wagon, nice looking horses. I rode over near them on my way to the cook wagon.

A man and a woman were working there. I asked them where Harlen was. They pointed in the direction of the three mounted men. I took that to mean one of them must have been Harlen the foreman.

As I rode towards them, one was using hand gestures, big circles and pointing in several directions. Soon two of the riders rode off. The other headed in my direction.

He introduced himself as Harlen, boss around here. He had a funny way of talking, not like the Canadians, completely different.

I introduced myself and told him where I was from.

He said, "Let's get coffee at the wagon."

As we proceeded to the wagon, he said, "a farm boy, huh."

"Yeah," I said.

"You wouldn't be looking for a job, would you?"

"Well, actually I'm looking to buy some good horse stock."

He looked at me funny, "A boy like you got money?" .

"Not on me," I said, "but at home. Do you ever sell any of your horses?"

"Well, yes we do, after the roundup and delivery to the rail head. We cull the herd and try to sell what we can up here and take the rest back to Texas for next spring's drive. Good grass up here but the winters are a man killer. How do you farmers keep your animals alive in the winter?"

"Lots of feed," I said. "Hay and grain, that's why we have to be farmers."

He laughed, "Yeah, I guess so. Cattlemen usually don't like settlers coming over and taking the free range. I don't know what's going to happen up here. We, the Circle C, had a station, more down towards

Milestown. But a few years back the Montana winter took them all."

"Before that, there were hundreds of outfits running free range cattle up here. We lost ninety percent that one year, what a loss. So now we're back to spring drive up, fall roundup, and spend the winters in Texas."

"How far is it to Texas?" I asked.

"Near on one thousand miles," he said.

"Wow, how long to drive a herd up here?"

"More than a month, sometimes two. But you got to know we don't have much winter down south. We can start the drive early and get up here just as the snow melts. Best grass anywhere, so the drive's worth it."

"How many have you got here?" I asked.

"About three thousand, but the Circle C has five other herds in Montana. One thing about the winter, it drove a lot of the outfits out of here. But there's a few ranches trying to start up here again. I guess they had to figure some winter feed some way."

"Yeah," I said, "but I don't know if the land'll be settled. Don't look like the country for it."

"Oh, I wouldn't say that," Harlen said. "There's settlers all through Colorado, Wyoming on land not as good this, but not so much winter. You all must be a special breed to survive here," he said.

"Say where'd you get those guns?"

"An outlaw auction," I said.

"What's that?"

"They caught the Missouri Kid rustling some horses. In the shootout, he got wounded. Then he died from infection, so they auctioned off his stuff to pay for the funeral. I wanted the stallion for my herd, but he went too high. So the sheriff talked me into buying his guns and tack."

"You must have some money hid to buy that stuff. Let me see one of those six shooters."

"Six shooters, yeah."

"Your Colts, they hold six rounds, right?

"Oh, I see."

71

"Wow, what is this?"

"They tell me its nickel plated because nickel doesn't rust so bad, and it's good for rough handling."

I took the revolver out so Harlen could shoot it. The 4" barrel made it light and balanced. I could tell Harlen was impressed. His Colt in his holster was a little worse for wear.

He asked if I had ever considered selling the revolvers. I didn't need them but liked having them.

"And that saddle. That looks like a Texas brand on there and real silver inlay. If you'd ever a mind, I'd give you good money for it all."

"Actually, I am more interested in horses," I said.

"Well boy, I got horses, real Texas blue blood quarter horses. If you got cash money like you say you have, we could make a deal."

My heart was pounding. These horses looked good, whatever real blue blood Texas quarter horses meant.

"Tell you what boy, come back in about two weeks with your money. Help us round up the herd and we'll make us a deal. Now these will be culled horses, the older ones, but still good stock mind you."

"Good enough for breeding?" I asked.

"The mares should be," he said.

"Some geldings and a stallion?" I asked.

"No," Harlen said. "These are working horses. With over three thousand head of wild steers, we don't have time to fight with stallions."

"Okay," I said. "I'll be back. I don't know how much rounding up I can do, but I'll have my money."

"And the saddle and guns," he added.

"Okay."

As I rode away, I couldn't help but notice how nimble and quick those quarter horses were. They were clearly a better horse than what I was riding. I couldn't wait to get on one.

Just to the northwest two figures sat low watching us. I didn't see any horses around, so I headed their way. One was an old man, rough looking, and the other was a younger boy with dark reddish copper skin and wearing leather. Were these Indians?

I heard so much about Indians but had never seen one. This used to be Indian country. I heard that all this land was Indian reservation at one time, but the white man kept moving in. Then when the Custer thing happened, they were restricted to even less land. My heart felt for them, a proud people that had all of this at one time. But now they were wandering the plains, homeless, looking bedraggled.

I couldn't imagine how they felt about the white man. I didn't know whether to try to talk to them or ride for my life. But neither seemed to have a weapon of any kind. They sat on their knees and seemed harmless. I waved at them and they smiled at me.

"Hi," I said. "Do you speak English?"

"Yes," the younger one said. He pointed "Do you like the horses?"

"Yeah," I said. "I'll try to buy some. What are you doing?"

"We need a horse."

The older one spoke in a language I didn't understand. He pointed and laughed a little.

"You have no horse?" I asked.

"They all died in the winter a few years back, so we walk now. We need a horse." They spoke with a lot of hand gestures and pointing, but the younger one could communicate in English.

I asked his name.

"Bob," he said.

"Bob, that's an American name," I said.

"Bob is what they called me at the mission school."

"Okay," I said. "My name is Bill."

"Hi." They both waved.

I was fascinated talking to them, never having met an Indian before. They didn't seem to be living up to their reputation of cut throat savages.

"His name is Noa."

"Noa," I repeated and Noa waved and started to talk and gesture.

I didn't understand so I asked Bob what language that was.

He looked at me surprised and said "English" like I was supposed to know that.

Noa laughed.

"He drinks a lot of whiskey, so his English isn't so good. We live over by the big river and we need a horse to hunt and pull the fish," Bob said.

Feeling for them, I asked if they had any money for a horse. They both looked at me puzzled.

"What is money?" Bob asked.

I was as surprised as they were.

I pulled out a dollar and said, "Money to buy a horse."

This seemed like a strange concept to them. I for the life of me couldn't figure out how these Indians expected to acquire a horse without money. So, I asked Bob if he had a job.

There was additional confusion and a big laugh from Noa. I was beginning to realize how different these Indians were. I could see them looking at the quarter horses with great admiration. For some reason I wanted to help them but didn't know what to do.

I told them where I was from and said if I could help them get a horse, let me know.

I said I had to go, but I will be back.

"Okay," Bob said. "See you."

"Okay," I waved.

They waved too.

Noa seemed to get a kick out of the whole thing, smiling and laughing the whole time. Like maybe he knew something I didn't. Like maybe they were going to steal in the night and get one of those horses.

The cowboys of Circle C seemed to pay them no mind and all of them wore, as the Texans called them, six shooters. A lot of the cowboys had rifles also, so I was still at a loss as to how Noa and Bob planned to get a horse.

CHAPTER 12

As I was riding home, I was planning my return trip. The more I thought about the quarter horses, the more I wanted them, even to the point that I decided to sell the horses I had to get them. I had to remember to hide my poker face when the Canadians returned. The quarter horses were more muscled and quicker than our horses. They were a breed that I thought would be of great value up here in cattle country.

I got home right at supper time. They all wanted to hear about my travels in outlaw country. They were disappointed when they heard that I hadn't seen one outlaw. They were fascinated to hear about the Indians.

"How did you know they were Indians?" Netty wanted to know.

"Well, they have darker, redder skin and they talk funny, different from the Texans and different from the Canadians," I said. "They wear leather clothes and seem to not know the concept of money and buying things."

Mom, who had been scoffing at my stories was starting to listen now.

She said, "They were different cultures. Different people live in different places, develop different ways of doing things, even different ways of acquiring things. Some societies live in a moneyless way of life. They barter and trade things and have no use for money."

"Wow, that would be different," Barney said.

Even Mom stayed up late hearing the whole story. She usually went to bed early and read her books, but I guess my adventure was more interesting.

The next morning, I told my dad I was going to sell out to the Canadians, take the money, and buy as many quarter horses as I could.

"I agree with your idea if it works out. Texans are different people. Those Indians are remnants of the Sioux and other tribes that defeated the 7th Calvary over there in Montana somewhere."

"Do you think they are dangerous now?" I asked. "They seemed friendly."

"Hard to say," Dad said. "I imagine there's dangerous Indians and friendly Indians, the same as all people. You're still young son and have a lot to learn."

"I'm seventeen and as big as any man now."

"That's the problem son. We were all young once and thought we knew it all. But the ways of the world will change that. The smart ones survive. The not so smart ones are the ones you hear about, who ventured over there and never came back."

Dad's words always seemed worth remembering. But Harlen seemed honest enough. He was a cattleman and not an outlaw.

I told Dad I would work extra hard to help with the keep of my horses, but he said not to worry about it. It was too good of money not to pass up.

So when the Canadians returned, they had only procured two older horses and were desperate for more.

"Three hundred fifty dollars you offered for the gelding?" I asked.

"Yes," he said.

"How many horses could you buy?" I asked.

Sensing I had some, Sem asked, "How many you got?"

Trying not to show my hand, "Seven," I said. "But I obviously can't sell them all."

"Three hundred fifty dollars for the breeders and gelding. Two hundred fifty dollars for the rest," Arvine said.

"Okay, let me think on it," I said.

As they were looking at the horses, I went to talk to Dad.

"Sell them all and use my horse to get the quarter horses."

I suggested we sell his and I keep one of mine for sale later. I would get him a quarter horse. He agreed. He was by now very interested in the so-called famous Texas quarter horses.

I was surprised when the Canadians had U.S. dollars. They decided to exchange the script themselves because most people didn't want that funny money.

I had just under two thousand dollars and Dad had three hundred fifty dollars. Dad suggested that I only take one thousand five hundred dollars with me in case things didn't work out, so the rest went into the bank.

I told everybody that I didn't know when I would be back. I was going to help with the roundup before we could buy the horses. Mom filled my big saddle bags with food and off I rode.

On the second day, it was too late to ride in, so I camped on a hill. I had gotten a warmer bed with me, sheep fleece, the same as my warm coat. The coyotes howled me to sleep. I was tired.

The sun was in my eyes when I awoke. My horse was standing over me and two Indians were on their haunches looking at me and my horse. I jumped up. Bob and Noa were there with big grins on their faces, like we got you. I could see Noa hid a knife under his shirt all right and figured Bob must have one too.

They smiled and waved at me. I had to lay there for a while to get my heart to stop pounding.

"Hi," I said. "How's it going?"

Noa started talking in his muddled tone and pointing off to the north. I looked up there to see two riders half a mile away.

"Who are they?" I asked.

Noa talked but Bob could tell I didn't understand.

"They follow you here and stop when you stop."

A shiver went up my back. Why was somebody following me? Could it be somebody who knew how much money I had on me . . . . outlaw trail! Nobody knew except my family and I was sure there was no problem there.

The Canadians surmised something was up when I sold all my horses. They figured I was headed to get more horses and that I had money on me. What was I going to do? Noa and Bob sat there wondering too.

After thinking on it, I decided that they weren't advancing on us. I got dressed, got my guns on, and said, "How about breakfast?"

Noa and Bob didn't know what I meant, but heartily ate the eggs and side pork. I was grateful for them. Maybe those two hadn't advanced on me because there were now three of us. I owed them. Their smiles were bigger with full stomachs. I decided to go to camp and see what happened.

Harlen was glad to see me.

"Wondered if you were going to show."

We started the roundup.

"I hate to tell you this, but your two friends are Indian."

"Yeah, I know," I said.

"We probably can't use Indians. Is that the only help you could find?"

Then I got an idea.

"No," I said. "My friends were following me. You could send somebody out to find them. They should be up north somewhere."

"Okay." He yelled at a nearby cowboy and sent him off to find the two riders that had been trailing me.

"Do we still have a deal?" I asked.

Harlen looked at those nickel-plated beauties and said, "We sure do. Two silvers a day plus all the grub you can eat."

"Okay."

"Grab a couple of fresh horses. I want you to join Frank and Lenny off to the north. Bring in as many as you can find."

"Can I take three?"

"Sure," he said.

I resaddled to the quarter horse and picked two more. After loading lots of grub in my saddle bags, I winked and nodded, headed north to Bob and Noa.

Over the hill, I promised them some money if they would help. Bob was excited. I nodded at the horse and Bob jumped on bareback. I didn't even see Noa get on, but there he was. They both grabbed the horses' mane and headed out.

Those quarter horses were the most trained animals I'd ever been on. Bob and Noa seemed to handle them perfectly with no bridle or saddle. For two people with no horses, I could tell they knew what they were doing. Bob and Noa's grins were the widest when they were on horseback.

We proceeded north and began rounding up the steers, all with Circle C brand. We brought in seventy some head. Frank said Lenny would have to stay and hold them at the water hole, so they didn't wander off.

They knew I had the Indians helping me. They didn't seem to mind because we were getting the job done faster.

Two days later we had over three hundred head. Lenny thought we had gotten every steer we could find, so we headed them back into camp.

Harlen was pleased. He had two cowboys counting the herd and we came within twenty some of the total that they brought there. The best count to date.

He thanked us.

I said, "Thank you, boss."

Harlen was big and dark. He had an imposing demeanor. I never called anyone boss before, but Harlen was the boss. Running this rough shod outfit required a man you didn't want to fool with.

I asked Harlen who owns Circle C? What was the guy's name?

No one name, a bunch of people. I didn't need to know. Just do my job and I would get paid. Don't worry about anything else. Wow, I thought. That was a touchy subject.

We were holding the cattle until the rest of the roundup was finished.

I asked one of the cowboys who owned the Circle C.

He looked at me and said, "Good question. As near as I have heard it is a bunch of investors from back east. There are no ranchers anymore. It all seems to be some monied people from the east somewhere, but we all get paid and nobody asks any questions."

I could see that the head man had to be tough. Some of the cowboys were rough and needed a strong hand to keep them in line.

The next day we headed the cattle southeast toward the railhead. I told Harlen there was a new rail to the north, but he said that the cattle were already contracted on this line.

"You have to help us get them across the big river and then we can settle up."

"Thanks," I said.

In late fall the river was low and easy crossing for the cattle.

Harlen took me aside and we culled fifteen horses out of the herd. He said these would bring two hundred fifty dollars in Texas. He could tell that I didn't believe him.

"I like you, kid. We did good. One thousand five hundred dollars, all your wages, and the rig. I know you had the Indians help so I'm adding a few dollars for them. I'll throw in an old saddle so you can ride home in style.

Okay, that was the deal, but I needed to keep my rifle.

"Why?" he asked.

"I'm far from home with these horses. I need one gun. I can trade it to you next time. The rifle is not nickel so it's not as unique as the revolvers."

"Actually, it is," he said. "It's a 26" barrel and I didn't know they even made such a thing."

"Okay," I said. "I'll be back with it next year, if you bring me up a quarter stallion."

"Wow, that would be a tough one kid. I wouldn't know where to get one."

"There has to be quarter stallions somewhere," I said.

"Yeah, but you might have to go all the way to Texas to find one. I think all the horse ranches geld them all except for what they need."

"Okay."

I thanked him. We shook and agreed to meet next year.

CHAPTER 13

I realized I didn't have any money to pay Bob and Noa. They both sat on their horses, big smiles, looking at me, like where to now boss.

I was trying to figure my way through this problem when Bob said, "We take your horses to your ranch now, okay?"

"Yeah, if you could help me, that would be great. I could pay you then. Don't you have to check in with your families or something?"

The looked at each other, confused.

"Can you help me take the horses home now?" I asked.

Noa was talking and pointing.

"What's he saying?" I asked.

"We're ready to take the horses."

"Okay, great. I just thought you might need to tell somebody where you are."

We headed them out. Apparently, that was another Indian thing, wandering off from your people and coming back whenever. I wondered if their families back home ever missed them or wondered where they were. I wondered if Noa and Bob were like the white guys that ventured west and were never seen again. A different culture, I guess.

The next day Noa was on the left, Bob right forward, and I was to the side rear. It was late fall and no snow. The streams were very low or dry and the sloughs were dried up to alkali. I hadn't planned on this. We were also low on food, but the Indians didn't complain. The quarter horses were used to herding and the going was good except for the water and food situation.

We were trudging along when I heard a loud whistle. I looked around and Noa was waving at me from the other side of the herd. He made several hand gestures then put up two fingers and pointed north. I rode out away from the dust and stood in my stirrups. Sure enough, two riders were way out there. I gave Noa the thumbs up and rode hard to catch Bob, who was laughing hard. I looked at him and he gave me the thumbs up.

"What was so funny?"

"What is this?" his thumbs were up.

"You don't know?" I asked.

He only laughed.

I said, "That's okay or I understand. What's so funny about that?"

"Nothing," Bob said. "I didn't know white men had sign language."

"Well, maybe that's the only one."

Bob put his thumb up and said, "Okay, okay."

I think he got it.

Bob asked if I saw the two riders.

"Yes," I said.

"Noa seems to think they are staying with us."

"Does he think they are the same two as before?"

Bob gestured to Noa and he waved back.

"Doesn't know, but maybe."

"What could we do?"

Bob said, "We could pull up in a draw and watch the herd from the hills, a good vantage point, and see what happens."

These Indians were smarter than I gave them credit for. I was very glad for the company of Bob and Noa now. If I had been alone, would these guys have tried to jump me?

There was three of us, but only one gun. I was now so glad I hadn't let that rifle go. I learned a lesson. Never be out here without being armed.

We staked the horses in the ravine and each took up a different position on the hills. We waited a long time, but nothing happened. Later the moon came out and the coyotes started to howl. I fell asleep a couple of times but tried to stay awake. Then there was some strange hooting in with the coyote howls. Somebody was running around. It was Bob.

"No riders around now. Time to sleep. I'll stay with the horses," he said.

"Okay, let me know if anything else pops up."

He smiled and gave me the thumbs up.

We awoke to a calm sunny morning, still tired from last night's escapade. Fresh water and food were getting to be a problem. With no remedy in sight, we pressed on.

I was starting to recognize the country when the horses wanted to veer right off the trail. I knew we were less than a day's ride from home. Bob and I were trying to keep the horses on track, when Noa started pointing to the south. After several hand gestures, Bob came over to me and said, "Water that way."

Okay, I thought and gave Noa a thumbs up. He laughed and gave me a thumbs up back. Within two miles, we came to a ravine with several acres of bright green grass. It looked so out of place compared to the brown late fall colors surrounding us.

"The horses smell the water," Bob said.

The horses dove in. We could then see the water standing under the grass. They weren't eating the grass but drinking the water under it. Some of them laid down and rolled in it. A spring was seeping out of the hillside just like our north pasture back home, but this was good water, running out over several acres on the bottom.

Noa was waving and pointing from the other side of the herd. A small group of antelope had been at the water but were now standing off in the distance. Bob waved to follow him. We laid down just over the ridge, just in time. The antelope charged over the ridge so close I couldn't miss. They were so close together that I just flock shot, and Bob gave me the thumbs up.

Noa popped over the hill bareback, riding as skillfully as anybody with a saddle. He had directed the antelope right at us. Now we had food and water. These Indians never wavered or complained as if they knew we would sooner or later find food and water.

I could see where we were now, and not far from home. Bob and Noa set to work building a fire, cutting strips of meat from the antelope, and starting to dry it. The antelope was a young one, only ¾ grown, so the meat should be good.

I was antsy to get home being so close, but the Indians and horses were settling in for the day. I guess they were home, I thought. This was it. Wherever food and water were, was home.

One more night sleeping on the ground was worth it for my biggest prize I had ever attained, fifteen Texas quarter horses. This was something nobody else in this country had and most of them were breeders. But of course, I still didn't have a stallion.

I was beginning to realize that the stud horse situation was beginning to be a problem. How far was I going to have to go? Texas perhaps?

Bob was tending to the cooking and Noa was tending to two of the horses that were somewhat lame. I had definitely gotten the lower end of the herd, but there were some fine animals there.

Noa was treating the injured legs with mud, which surprised me. But I had no other idea of what to do.

CHAPTER 14

The horses and the Indians were right. We needed the rest, not so much because we had come so far, but we hadn't had good food and water. To travel hard across this country, you need good nutrition and water.

This was different country from Dakota. The resources were fewer and farther between. A man out here without a horse would surely not survive. I realized I had a lot to learn and was surprisingly learning it from the supposedly savage Indian. When you think about it, the Indians had survived here for centuries, albeit with the now absent buffalo.

I was saddened. I thought the buffalo was a big, majestic animal. I couldn't figure out why anybody would want to exterminate them. I guessed it was to make room for the cattle, cattle owned by absentee eastern owners. I loved the wide open western lands free for exploration and whatever. I couldn't wait to return.

Bob and Noa were on the hill looking and pointing at something.

When I got there, Bob said, "tepee rings."

There were large circles of rocks. Bob explained that they held down the edge of the buffalo skins of the tepees. There were several of them. The Indians had been here before. Some of the rocks were half-buried, so it had been a while ago, but they had been here.

We headed for the final drive home. A short time later Noa pointed and gestured.

Bob said, "Buffalo wallow."

The buffalo had been here also.

The horses had been refreshed, so the trip home was short. We got there later in the day. My brothers and especially my dad were impressed. But not as impressed as seeing Indians for the first time.

They were amazed how well Bob spoke English. They peppered him with questions, his schooling, and where he lived. Then I noticed Bob and my sister staring at each other. I couldn't tell if it was admiration or shock. I thought of what my mother said, culture shock.

I couldn't believe this was the first white women Bob had seen, but I was sure he was the first Indian Netty had seen. Mom grabbed Netty to make supper.

I started saddling the quarter horses to show them to Dad and my brothers. Dad had never seen such capable strong horses, but then asked where the stallion was.

"Don't have one," I said.

"I think it would pay you to keep this pure blood line," Dad returned.

"Yeah, I know, but I might have to go all the way to Texas to get one."

"Texas," he yelled.

"Yeah, these are blue blood Texas quarter horses and I guess that's where all the breeding ranches are."

"Texas," Dad repeated.

Barney and Carl said, "Go for it."

Carl asked, "What does blue blood mean?"

I shrugged.

Dad said, "I guess it's linked to the fact that this lineage of horse makes them superior, just like our pure-bred Herefords.

"Okay," Bob said. "We go to Texas to get the stallion."

We all laughed.

"You want to go?"

"Yes," Noa wanted to go and gave a thumbs up.

Wow I thought, one thousand miles, but we didn't have a lot to do over the winter except feed livestock. I asked Dad. He said he and Mom were going to Minnesota on the train to visit.

"That would be a good chance to pick up some more horses over there."

"We hadn't planned that. Besides, we have about all the horses we can feed right now," he said.

"I'm going to sell all but the best breeders to the Canadians and maybe we can get a stud horse over there."

Dad didn't look too excited about wrangling horses on the way home.

I said, "I could go with and bring the stock back while you visit and can come back later."

"Okay, but what will you do with the Indians?"

"I'll send them home tomorrow."

"Okay," we agreed.

I told Bob and Noa the plan, but they didn't seem concerned one way or the other. I got the feeling they liked being with the horses as much as anything, so I told them I would try to get away and we would go south this winter to find horses.

Both gave a thumbs up and big smiles.

I gave them their money and we left the next day. We stopped in Williston at the big mercantile. I bought Bob and Noa new white man clothes. They both wanted a blanket. I also bought them boots and broad brimmed hats.

Bob said, "Good to buy Noa something, otherwise he would spend his money on whiskey."

"Do you think he would be up for the trip south?" I asked.

Bob looked at me funny, "Why not?"

"How old is he? His face is pretty wrinkled."

"He's only about thirty five," Bob said.

"Are you sure?" I asked. "He looks a lot older than that."

Bob shrugged and said, "Whiskey and smoking."

"Thirty five," I repeated.

Bob shrugged and Noa gave a thumbs up and laughed.

The mercantile had a new Winchester rifle, but it was only a .22 long rifle. The clerk said it was for the new smokeless powder.

"Do you have one of the .44 - .40 caliber?" I asked.

"No, the .30 Winchester caliber is the new rifle cartridge, and we haven't received our order yet."

We picked up some eating supplies and left. We went to Bob's people the next day. They had a big camp on the north bank of the big river, what white people call the Missouri River. Their dwellings were scattered among the trees in the hills. They settled there to fish, the only thing they could do after the buffalo were gone.

Bob's Dad fished the big river and smoked them. He had become an expert at it. He knew what kind of wood to use to flavor the fish. I had not eaten very many fish before, but this was good.

I was surprised to find out Noa had a wife and a lodge. He didn't seem too concerned about leaving her for long periods of time. I guess that was natural here.

Bob's Dad was named Walker, short for long walker. Despite his name, he was in desperate need of a horse. Walker told of the bad winter five summers ago and how they lost all their stock and had to eat them to stay alive. Now he caught many fish and smoked them for the long winter. I decided to leave one of my horses there for them to use until I got back and we headed south for horses. They gave me fish for my trip home. I thanked them and left.

I was going to make it all the way home that next day, so I let my horse have his own head. To my surprise he led us back to the springs. I believe horses smell good water. I was beginning to like the place. I was even thinking how I could build corrals and a shack there. The antelope returned, but I had plenty of fish.

CHAPTER 15

Back at the farm Mom and Dad informed me that Netty was going with us to visit the relatives in Minnesota. Barney said that Sem and Arvine had been by and were very interested in some of the quarter horses.

"Great," I said. "I hope they get here before we leave."

I asked Barney if he and Carl could handle the place while we were gone. He scoffed at me as if it was an insult.

Carl said, "We are bringing all the animals home anyway, so we can watch them closer here."

Good idea, I thought, with the hoof prints we had seen with our cattle out in the north pasture.

"We're going to be crowded around here. I hope the Canadians get here so we can thin out the herd."

The next day all four of us headed up to bring our cows and sheep home. Dad, Barney, and Carl were all on quarter horses, so we were about to find out how they did around the cows.

As we got to the pasture two new horsemen were waiting for us, Sem and Arvine. Sem was on a lighter colored horse. I was sure it was not one of the horses we saw in Montana. They couldn't have switched horses today.

"Howdy, greetings, did your brothers tell you we had been by to check out your new horses?"

"Yeah," I said. "What do you think?"

"Very nice," Arvine added.

"Genuine blue blood Texas quarter horses."

"Where did you get these?" Sem asked.

I was caught. What could I say? I couldn't tell him I got these just across in Montana or did he already know?

So, I said, "Texas, of course."

They both got a laugh out of that.

"Well, down that way anyway. Follow us back to the farm and I'll show you how they handle cattle."

They didn't let on that they thought any funny business was going on or at least their poker faces were perfected.

I could tell they were impressed. The quarter horses kept the cows and sheep perfectly, bunched all the way back, and guided them through the corral gates. I jumped off the one I was on and ground hitched her there and she didn't move.

Sem and Arvine were down and closely inspected the new horses, while we finished closing the gates.

"We've never seen horses quite like this before. How many do you want to sell?"

"I want to keep the best breeding prospects and cull the rest."

After looking them all over, they asked, "What kind of money are we talking?"

I pointed to the five I wanted to sell and said, "I figure three hundred fifty U.S. cash a piece for these."

"You got a couple of partially lame ones there," Arvine noticed.

Before I could say anything, Sem offered three hundred fifty U.S. for eight, which included one of the lame ones.

Did I want to let some of my breeding stock go? I needed more money for the horse buying trip to Minnesota. I was keeping the best breeders I figured so I shook.

"U.S. dollars," I repeated.

Sem dug out his money and started counting. I asked Carl to get some paper from the house for the bill of sale.

After the Canadians left with their new horses, I thoroughly inspected their hoof prints, and they didn't resemble any of the prints of the mysterious riders.

I was very relieved that Sem and Arvine's prints didn't match, but that fact didn't completely eliminate them. Their money had always been good, and they must be successful because they kept coming back.

Within the week, we were sitting on the train headed to Minnesota. They were all dressed up. I had my best blue jeans and cleanest shirt. Netty commented that I had a suit.

"I know," I said, "but I'm not going to church. I'm going to get the horses and head back home. You all can do the visiting this time. I'm getting these horses and if I don't get a stallion this time, I'll be heading for Texas."

"You going to take the Indians with you?" Dad asked.

"Yes."

"They seem to be friendly," Mom said, "but can you trust them?"

"Already have, Mom," without telling them about the two riders shadowing us in Montana.

I said, "We took turns standing guard on the horses at night. With two of them and one of me, they probably could have taken the horses at any time. I met Bob's parents and Noa's wife. They're just horsemen like me. They lost all of their animals a few years back, so I am trying to help them get a couple of horses back."

"Yeah, the storm of 87- 88. I heard about it," Dad said.

"Those two are a couple of the best horsemen that I have ever seen. Noa trained and broke horses for a living"

"Yeah," Dad said. "He really looked like he knew what he was doing around them."

"Are you sure he's not too old?" Netty asked.

"He's only thirty five," I said.

They all laughed.

"No," I said. "It's true."

"How'd he get so wrinkled and dark?"

I shrugged and said, "I guess it's just tough country they live in over there in Montana."

"Yeah," Dad said. "I think it is."

"Do you think that state will ever get settled over there, Dad?"

"If they ever clean up the outlaws, I think so. Where we are wasn't a lot different a few years back, but now look at it. Settlers everywhere."

"Yeah, and law and order," I added.

CHAPTER 16

Netty was excited. She had never ridden the train before and was too young to remember her grandparents from the last visit. I was glad they were going to do all the visiting. I could get the horses and head home.

We had a one day layover in Grand Forks, so we went to the big mercantile store there. It had everything, a lot more than any of the stores back home. Walking around, I eventually found the gun department. They had a whole rack of Winchesters. There was a wall poster with advertising for the new Winchester .30 WCF smokeless round. That was the funniest bullet I ever saw, tall and kind of bottle shaped.

The clerk said, "It was the first bullet made for the Winchester 94 rifle use only."

"Looks kind of big to me."

"That is so it can hold more powder. See the big chamber? With more powder, the lead is faster and stronger. The faster it is, the straighter it will fly, so you can hit things out there at a greater distance."

I was impressed and interested. Harlen said he wanted my old rifle.

The clerk handed me one of the rifles that fit the new .30 WCF cartridge. It was shiny and had a new, beautiful wood stock. The price tag said seventeen dollars, a lot more money.

"It has to be a better, stronger steel to hold greater pressure," the clerk said.

Yeah, that made sense.

I was carrying two thousand five hundred dollars in my pocket. When I thought of that, seventeen dollars didn't seem so bad.

"You'll have to save your money for a long time to get that, huh."

I wanted to show him my money, but then remembered to never show your money. I wandered off to think about it.

Next was the saddle department. I had never seen a new saddle before. Would I look good on one of those?

The clerk said, "Get on. It's on that rack for testing. You can sit on it."

I knew something was different as soon as I sat down. The top layer had a cushion under it. It was like sitting in a cushion chair at home.

"Fifty dollars, or forty dollars for one without the cushion."

I had been thinking there was going to be a lot of saddle riding to get to Texas and back. I didn't realize how hard and worn out those old two dollar used saddles were. Another thing to think about.

Next was the boot department. Riding boots, why would they be any different from any other boot?

"The high heel," the clerk said.

Yeah, they were a lot higher than I had ever seen, but why?

"So your foot won't go through the stirrup and catch your leg if you are bucked off. You could get dragged."

Tried them on, soft leather. They were nothing like I had ever had, twenty dollars. I'm a horseman, I thought.

"I'll take 'em."

These boots were so nice. I couldn't stop thinking about the saddle or rifle.

I walked around the whole store and couldn't believe all that was in there. I found a small area with hundreds of books.

The Wild West, a small one stated. I started reading it. It turned out to be about cowboys, Indians, and outlaws. I couldn't put it down, ten cents. *True Tales of the West* another said. *Jesse James and his Gang*, *Wyatt Earp*, *Wild Bill Hickok*, *Billy the Kid*, and *Kit Carson*.

"They're like penny dreadfuls," the clerk said. "All true stories of the west for only ten cents.

It dawned on me that I could read these while I was trail riding. I picked out nine of them.

"You can find another for an even dollar," the clerk said.

Annie Oakley, a girl in the west that could shoot.

I wanted it all and none of this stuff was available back west. After thinking about it, I could trail the horses home and save more money instead of riding the train. More than enough to pay for it all.

I bought several large grain bags. I had the boots and books. Next was the Winchester, seventeen dollars. But then I saw a shorter one on the rack.

"Saddle carbine," the clerk said, handing it to me.

Shorter and lighter with a ring on the side.

"That's to tie it to your saddle."

It was two dollars less at fifteen dollars. The bullets were one dollar and fifty cents, same as the .44 - .40, but when I got them, there were only twenty rounds instead of fifty.

I was hooked now. I wanted it. Five boxes, then to the saddle. It fit the largest grain sack.

"You need a bridle," the clerk said.

Matching new tanned leather, five dollars.

"Do you need a slicker? You want to keep dry and warm on the trail."

"And a big saddle bag," I said.

"Don't have any that big, but the leather man down the street can make you anything you want."

Special oil for the saddle and boots. Special oil and cleaner for the Winchester. All came out to less than one hundred dollars. It would have cost me more than that to get the horses home on the train. Three bags were full.

I found Mom, Dad, and Netty. They couldn't resist and made several purchases. I handed them each a grain sack. After we paid for everything, the clerk said the wagon would be by to take our stuff to the train station. They asked what I had bought?

"A new pair of boots and these," I showed them the books, trying to keep their attention away from the expensive saddle and gun I bought. Netty picked up *Anne Oakley* and started to read it.

Mom said sarcastically, "Oh these are going to be educational."

Netty couldn't put the book down, so I told her to keep it. I could read it later. Then Dad picked one up.

"Go ahead, I'll read that one later too," I said, handing one to Mom. "You were trying to get me to read more."

"Yeah, but this is not what I had in mind."

Dad just smiled and kept reading. We were all so enthralled in our books that we almost missed our stop. We ended up having to hire a wagon to haul our stuff across the river to Grandpa's house. They were too busy talking to notice Uncle Ned and I slip off to look at the horses, five mares and one gelding.

"These are great," I said. "I'll take them, but I still need a stallion."

"They're tough to come by," Ned said. "Most are gelded young. I found a draft stud but that's not what you are looking for."

"Yeah, I'm looking for a high-quality rider. How about that black stallion your neighbor had?"

"I think they still have it," he said. "Let's ride over and find out."

As we rode up to the neighbor's farm, we could see the black stallion out in the pasture.

"Still haven't been able to geld him yet?" I asked.

"No, we kept him because we hoped he would have done some breeding, but he seems too hyper and wild for even that."

"Would you consider selling him?"

"We wouldn't want somebody to get hurt by this horse, so we've decided to put him down," the neighbor said.

"I think I could handle him if you would let me try."

By then the father came out and said, "If you can get a bridle on him and lead him out of that corral without him biting you, he's yours."

I watched the cowboys out west handle wild horses. We got the black stallion into the corral. I put the Hackamore in my hind pocket. I spread the lasso on the ground holding onto the end of it. I then waved the grain sack at his face. He backed up slowly until his back legs were standing on the lasso. I pulled it hard, just as his legs got tangled in the rope. I jumped at him with the sack.

He couldn't get his back legs under him and he went down. Before he realized what was happening, I jumped on his head and covered his face and eyes with the grain sack. With Uncle Ned's help we put the Hackamore over the sack, holding it over his eyes. He could still bite so we put a feed bag over his muzzle. He laid there thrashing his tangled legs. I let him struggle as we talked.

When he tired and started to calm down, I pulled the lasso off his legs and put it over his head. He laid there, disoriented, unable to see. I started rubbing him down and talking to him. I rubbed his neck and steadied him and helped him up. He was confused. He had never been in this situation before. I talked to him and started to lead him. He finally followed, not knowing what else to do.

They were all amazed. He couldn't bite, run, or kick. He was had. He shook his head trying to get the

Hackamore and sack off his head, but it didn't work, so he followed as I led him out of the corral.

"We could geld him now," I told the neighbors.

"No," the father said. "I wouldn't know if we could still trust him. A deal is a deal, he's yours."

"I could pay you something for him."

"Just taking him off our hands is enough," he said. "It'll save us the price of a bullet. If you'd let us know how he turns out, we'd be interested."

"I will definitely do that," I said.

CHAPTER 17

When Dad saw us returning with the black stallion, he came out running.

"Be careful," I said. "We had to return the feed muzzle and he bites."

"Yeah," Dad said, "and he can't see either."

"Well, that's a safety precaution," I said.

"Oh, what did you get yourself into now, kid?"

"Oh, he'll be okay," I said. "My first stallion."

Dad, Uncle Ned, Grandpa, and I sat on the porch drinking coffee and watching the horses.

"I'm leaving tomorrow early," I announced.

"Well, boy, you're always in a hurry," Grandpa said. "Barely taking time to sit and visit."

"Barney and Carl are home alone, and they are handling the place for the first time by themselves. Besides, they're having to take care of my horses, so I feel guilty not helping."

I actually wanted to get out on my new saddle, boots, and rifle and try them out. And I had a wild stallion to boot.

"You and Grandma could ride the train over anytime and visit us," I said.

"Good idea," Dad said.

"Oh, we'll be there at some point," Grandpa said. "I can't wait to see how you come out with that stallion and I want to see those famous blue blood Texas quarter horses. See if all that Texas bragging is up to what it says it is."

Early the next morning, Uncle Ned helped me saddle and tether the horses. We tied the stallion between two of the biggest horses. I bought two old used saddles and we tied him to each of the saddle horns between the two horses. There wasn't much he could do but follow.

He tried to bite the horse's head. I got another grain sack and put it over his muzzle and worked it under the Hackamore so he couldn't bite or get it off. So, I now had him under control, I thought.

They waved goodbye. Netty waved with the Annie Oakley book she couldn't put down.

I crossed the river and went right on past the train station. The agent looked at my strange conglomeration of horses and probably thought, what's that kid up to now? I was almost nineteen, not a kid anymore. I wanted to tell him. Barney would be twenty one soon and old enough to homestead. Most of the good farming homesteads were gone.

Barney squatted on one just five miles to the west. It was about half good farm ground, but the rest was hilly, so we decided I would help him fence it if I could run some horses there. We built a small barn on the place with some corrals, so he could show it was being squatted on.

As soon as I was out of sight, I unbagged my new saddle, saddled up the gelding, tied the new rifle to the saddle horn, and headed straight west. I now knew to get around the big lake before turning north.

The restless stallion kept the horses trotting. This actually wasn't good because I couldn't read my book. Eventually they tired and slowed down.

The books were fascinating. They had all kinds of stories about what had happened out west. This piqued my interest and I really wanted to get out there and ride the areas where all these things happened.

I wasn't having any trouble finding farms to buy room and board for me and the horses. Most people wanted to visit and were most interested about the lands further on west, so I seemed to be welcome everywhere.

The stallion couldn't eat through the sack muzzle, but water would seep in and he could drink. He was running low on energy and was a lot more docile, just like I liked him. I didn't care now. I was either going to break him or starve him. If he was going to be too hard to train, he was not going to be a stud anymore. But he was too hardheaded to understand that.

We were calling him Blacky, the only thing we could think to call him. I doubled the reigns by adding a second rope from the Hackamore to the saddle horns.

I finished the first book and started on the second. There was an outlaw in there by the name of Black Bart, because he always wore black. Wow, I thought, Black Bart.

I looked at Blacky and said, "You are now Black Bart, you outlaw."

I couldn't believe how the books made the time pass by. I was well over half-way home, then it happened. I recognized the place, the mule skinner. He was out pulling stumps with a team. I was impressed.

"Did you pull all those stumps with those mules?"

He recognized me, "Sure did sonny."

Right away he went into his sales pitch. "I've got a special team just for you, less than three years old and just trained to the harness. Still two hundred fifty dollars, just like I told you. We'll hitch them up and I'll demo them."

"I'm not really the farmer, my dad is, and he was the one that said we should get a team of mules someday."

"Yeah, well, you try to get a good set of draft horses for anything like two hundred fifty dollars and see what you get."

"Can you ride them?" I asked.

"Sure can, been trained to. These aren't just trained to the harness."

"Well, I don't know, awfully funny looking with these big ears." Ugly, I thought, not wanting to say it.

"Boy, that's an awfully nice saddle and boots you got. Looks to me you could buy these mules easy and present them to your Dad."

I went to inspecting them. They were strong, muscled animals that looked like they could pull a load. I wondered what the Canadians would pay for something like this. They seemed to be desperate for any kind of horsepower. So I don't think they would mind at all to have these, especially for the price.

"Tell you what," he said, "buy 'em and if they don't work out for you, bring 'em back and I'll give you your money back."

"Okay," I said. "Let me stay here and I'll think on it overnight."

"Put you right up," he said.

We took the mules he had in the barn out, so we could put my horses in there and then he put big steaks on the grill. Wow, he was a salesman. I then proceeded to learn everything about a mule that anyone could ever want to know.

"That's all they use down in Missouri. I know, 'cuz that's where I'm from."

How could I guess. The night seemed to go on forever. We saddled the mules and tied the stallion between them.

"Those mules will keep that stallion in line, you just watch."

So, with all tethered together, I headed out, mules and all.

Cleg waved the two hundred fifty dollars at me and said, "If anybody else needs any mules up your way, just send them down. Oh, and they love carrots," he yelled.

Ha, I finally got away. This was going to be interesting. Any self-respecting horseman wouldn't want to be seen with these. Oh well, I was nearing home and would be camping out now anyway. The stallion would try to bite at the mules, but they fought back. One bit him on the muzzle so hard it drew blood. That ripped a hole in the grain bag and Black Bart could eat again. I didn't care because I'd be home soon.

I continued with my books. I camped that night. The next night I'd be at Uncle Ed's place.

I was getting used to the mules. They had a different temperament than a horse. By now I admitted they were easy to work with and had some good qualities. When I pulled into Uncle Ed's place, he came out laughing.

"What have you got now, boy?"

"Mules and a blind-folded black stallion."

"Let's put them up and you can tell me the whole story."

Uncle Ed inspected the animals as we put them up and fed them. I was surprised how he looked over the mules.

"Heard a lot about them but never seen them before."

"We will find out," I said, "Dad was the one who wanted to try them, so here they are."

The next day it snowed. I almost forgot about winter coming on. It could do that. One day nice, then the first snow squall hits.

The stallion was eating again through the hole in the muzzle and was getting his energy back, so I had my hands full dealing with him and the snow.

I made it home only running into one mud hole. The exact trail was hard to see in the snow, which was over six inches deep by now. Carl and Barney were watching for me. They came running, barking dogs, chickens, and all. Not even hardly saying hi, they went to looking at the animals. Barney got a big smile on his face when he saw the mules.

"So, Dad won that argument," he said.

"Actually, he doesn't know about them yet."

Carl was staring at the new rifle.

"First thing," I said, "the stallion is wild and he bites, so let me handle him."

"That's why you got him tied between those two mules?

"Yes."

"So, you got a stallion, but he's wild?" Barney asked.

"Actually dangerous," I said, "keep away from Black Bart."

"Black Bart, where'd you get that name?" Carl asked.

"Help me unload and I'll show you."

We had animals everywhere, barn was full, shed was full, corrals were all full of horses now with the cattle and sheep out in the home pasture, not to mention the pigs and chickens. We got everything put up, fed, and hauled my stuff to the house. Barney brought the new saddle in so he could look at it.

I handed one of the books to Carl and he said, "That's where Black Bart came from." He sat down and started to read.

"How much for that saddle?" Barney asked.

So I told him about the big mercantile back east and all the stuff for sale in it.

"They sell you stuff you didn't even know you needed."

"I am very glad he mentioned the slicker. I'd be awfully wet now if I didn't have it. How have you two been doing home alone?"

"Great," Barney said. "We can handle everything easy. Except we found out we couldn't cook as good as Mom. Mom and Dad wrote they are going to stay another week or so."

"I can believe that," I said. "I didn't know we had so many relatives back there and they all want to know what it's like out here."

CHAPTER 18

At breakfast we talked about how many animals we had on the place and whether we would have enough feed and hay for all of them if it's a bad winter. Barney said that the Canadians had been by while I was gone and seemed to indicate that they would be back. I would definitely have to let some of my stock go or buy some expensive feed.

I decided to write to Dad to tell him about the mules and ask what we should do. I obviously hadn't planned properly. To make things worse, the snow kept piling up.

We fed the stock and I worked on training Black Bart. We had a saddle and bridle on him all the time. We also added weight to the saddle. I gave him reduced feed and wore him down by backing him around the deep snow.

I used a two-foot-long stick to keep him from biting. One day while he was standing in almost belly deep snow, I jumped on him. He didn't know what to do. He tried to buck but with the deep snow it didn't work. I kept riding him in the deep snow. I eventually rode him to Colgan to get shoes on him.

Mom wrote back and said they were staying in Minnesota for Christmas. Dad suggested we sell some of the horses, but the Canadians had not returned, probably because of the weather. I was beginning to remember the stories of the winter of 87- 88 and how ninety percent of the stock had been lost.

The storms finally let up, but the snow was still deep. We borrowed a sleigh and went to Uncle Ed's for Christmas. Uncle Ed informed us that the train was not running because of the snow. There was no mail and no word from Mom and Dad.

Uncle Ed said we had to figure on feeding the livestock for at least three months. He didn't have as much livestock as we had and may have some extra feed to sell us.

No train and no word from our parents and no show of the Canadians. Winters here could be especially bad and, of course, worse if you weren't prepared for them.

I rode Black Bart every day now. We even got him shoed by tying each leg, one at a time, to get the job done.

About mid March, a single horse approached from the west. Two riders, Noa and Bob, both smiling said, "We go to Texas."

I laughed, "Too much winter. How did you get here?"

"The higher areas of the plains were blown clear of snow. No deep snow until Dakota."

They made out good with the horse to pull their fish net out of the ice hole in the big river.

"You don't need to help fish?" I asked.

"No, too many fish. We go to Texas."

"Too much winter, next year," I said. We need to keep the stock alive till spring grazing."

Bob and Noa stayed to help with the stock and coming calving.

When I showed them the new horses, they both laughed when they saw the mules.

Noa pointed and gestured saying something I couldn't make out.

"What language is that anyway?" Barney asked.

I looked at him and said, "English."

He looked at me funny and walked away shaking his head.

I noticed Noa wearing moccasins again.

"What happened to his boots?" I asked Bob.

He shrugged, "probably whiskey."

I remembered my old boots and got them. They were too big for him but with his moccasins on, they were a perfect fit.

By mid April, the train started running again and Mom and Dad returned home without Netty. She was attending a girls' boarding school in Minnesota.

Dad was impressed with the five of us. We didn't lose any livestock, not even a calf or lamb. This was good because we heard of several animal losses across the two-state area.

Finally, the Canadians showed up. Their losses had been worse than ours. They needed both cattle and horses. The bad news was they didn't have as much money to pay for them.

Eager to thin the herd, Dad asked them to make an offer. I showed them the horses we wanted to sell. To my surprise they wanted the mules. Dad was reluctant to let them go but I said the mule skinner had plenty more.

Bob and Noa stayed and worked for us all summer. We didn't pay them much, but they mainly just took care of the livestock.

As spring progressed, Bart was eating well and after regaining his former strength he returned to his old ways, bucking, kicking, biting, and he seemed so wild that he didn't breed. I eventually borrowed Uncle Ed's stud horse to hopefully coax him along, but nothing.

Noa said, "The horse is crazy wild."

I asked if we should geld him. Noa was confused, he didn't understand gelding.

After explaining it to him he said, "But no breed?"

I shrugged. He shrugged back. We both laughed.

That summer the Canadians eventually got enough money to buy the horses, mules, and ten cow calf pairs I wanted to sell, but for less money than planned.

I asked Arvine if the horse market was going to be able to sustain itself.

"We will always need horses," he said, "but I don't know what the market will be. The settlers have slowed down after last winter's harsh snow."

Sem was looking at Black Bart and said, "one thousand U.S. money."

"One thousand dollars?" I repeated.

Noa laughed and said in a low voice, "We go to Texas," and pointed south.

We both laughed.

"It might take me a week or two to get the money, but yes, one thousand dollars."

Wow, that was a surprise with the market being so low. I didn't know what to say. I had no intentions of selling Bart, but one thousand dollars for one horse was unheard of.

"Think about it, we'll be around," Sem said.

"Okay. Bye."

After they left, we went in to eat. I told Dad about the offer.

He said, "I'm not really surprised. I'll bet they're desperate to breed horses there. With what they're paying down here, they need to breed their own stock. Son, you've done good. Everybody around here has been concerned with raising cattle, pigs, and sheep, like back in Minnesota, not realizing the horse market potential of Canada. I've heard that the old outlaw trail in Montana used to bring a lot of stolen horses and cattle to the Canadian markets."

"We only stumbled onto it by accident the day Arvine and Sem rode by," I said. "But now we are money rich and horse poor, except for the few breeder quarter horses I kept and Bart."

"Yeah," he said. "Why don't you go over to the mule skinner and get another team. I know how you feel about them, but Arvine and Sem said they worked out great and indicated they may be interested in more. Besides we're short on horsepower around here without them."

I agreed, so off I went on one of the quarter mares. I didn't want to fool with Bart. Besides Noa was still working with him. I, of course, took my book with for the trail. The more of these books I read, the more I became fascinated with the west. I was for sure planning a trip to Texas this winter. Dad would be home, so I wouldn't be needed so much. And with the Canadians paying up to one thousand dollars U.S. for a good stud horse, it would be worth the trip.

I saw only two mules in the corral as I rode into the farm. I dismounted and kept reading and eating some jerky from my saddle bag. After a while, the skinner came riding in on another mule.

"See, I knew you'd be back, but I got to tell you I only got three left. Bad winter and people lost stock.

These aren't as good a set as I sold you, but they're still three hundred fifty dollars, cause it's the last team I got and one hundred dollars for Bessy here. She's a little old but got a lot of work left in her. The others were great, right?"

Finally, I got a word in, "Yeah, two hundred fifty dollars," I offered.

"Oh no," he said. "I sold all the others for three hundred fifty dollars or better because of all the stock everybody lost."

He knew he had me. I wouldn't have ridden all the way over here if I wasn't going to buy.

"Well, I only need the team, so . . ."

He cut me off and said, "Three hundred fifty dollars for all three. Besides, you need something else to ride home."

I looked at my horse and asked, "Why?"

"She's pregnant."

Surprised, I asked, "How do you know?"

"Boy, I know horses as well as mules and I'll bet she'll deliver."

I was elated. Was he right? Were all my mares pregnant? Or was he a good salesman. Suddenly, I had a really good feeling.

"Okay, three hundred fifty dollars."

I counted out three hundred fifty dollars. He unsaddled my horse and saddled Bessy. All his mules survived the winter.

He said, "I found out mules are tougher than horses. I have to give you old Bessy because I have to leave to go to Missouri for a new herd of mules."

"Wow, you go all the way to Missouri for the mules?"

"Yep, trail them back. No problem. Did I mention they like carrots? They'll follow you anywhere if you have carrots. I'll be back in a couple of months if you need more. I have the best Missouri mules in all of Dakota."

He was still talking when I waved and headed out.

I noticed we weren't covering as much ground as usual. Was he right? Were my horses pregnant? Was I finally going to be a successful horse breeder? I finished the last book and wondered where I could get more. Barney, Dad, and Carl were all reading them now.

Mom, not pleased with the content, was happy we were advancing our reading skills. I was so desperate for more books that I swung north to see if the mercantile in Crosby had any. I got a lot of stares coming into town on the mules, so I proceeded quickly to the general store. I only found seven that I hadn't already read.

There on display was a huge knife. Some guy makes them out of railroad springs. The clerk picked up the knife, pried a large box open and then sharpened it on a stone. He then shaved the hair on my arm. I was impressed.

"Five dollars, every mule skinner should have one," he said laughing.

"Okay, one dollar off for the joke," I said. "Do you have any real large saddle bags?"

"Not that big, but the leather goods man is just down the street."

"Okay," I said and left.

"It would take two hours to make," he said.

"Okay, I'll eat and be back."

I stabled the mules and mare and went to get something to eat. I still had a half hour to go, so I went back to the store where the clerk waved the big knife at me. I shopped around for a while and eventually walked out of there with some Winchester .30 ammo and a big new knife in a sheath on my belt. The saddle bags were five dollars but I thought it was worth it.

CHAPTER 19

Uncle Ed came walking out of his barn and said, "more mules."

"Yep, we already sold the others, so Dad had me go after these. We got the Indians working our stock, so we need another draft team. Want to get more hay and grain put up this year. May have another winter, you know."

We put up the horse and mules and went in to eat.

We were still talking the next morning when I finally said, "I gotta get these mules home and get them earning their pay."

My uncle laughed and waved.

"I sent you after two and you come home with three," Dad retorted.

"But for the price of two," I returned.

"Three hundred fifty dollars?" he asked.

"Yeah," I said.

He cooled his demeanor. He made me run the mules on the grinder. With extra "horsepower" and the extra moisture from the heavy snows, we put up more hay and grain than we ever had.

One evening after supper while Dad and I were out checking the stock, I told him I was going over to Montana to try and find Harlen to see if he had any extra quarter horses this year.

"Good idea," Dad said. "If we could get a pure-bred quarter horse herd started, we would have a unique product for a unique market."

"Yeah, if the Canadians recover enough to pay the price," I said.

"So far these horses have returned more than the farm and cattle put together."

"Yeah I know, I still plan to head to Texas as soon as I get Harlen's horses back here."

"You going to take the Indians with you?"

"Yes, they're the best horsemen I know. Besides who else would ride a thousand miles with me?"

"You're headed into some pretty unsettled country, so you better be able to trust the people you're riding with. This could be a unique, lucrative opportunity but it's not something to get killed or even hurt over."

"So, you think the west could be as bad as depicted in those dime novels?" I asked.

"I know Custer and the 7th Cavalry were all wiped out just over there in Montana somewhere. Wild Bill Hickok was shot from behind just down in southern Dakota somewhere. I've also heard that the shootout at the OK Corral actually happened. So yes, at least some of them are accurate."

"Don't you think that a lot of that is settled and over now? There are sheriff or law enforcement to cover all the territory by now?"

"I would think, but I don't think it's as settled as here. I'd be awfully careful. At nineteen years old, you have a lot to experience and learn yet."

148

I looked at Dad and said, "I get the message. I'll back out of any bad situation and head for home if things get bad."

He shook my hand as if welcoming me into a new world. But the west was calling. So the next week Bob, Noa, and I packed up. I decided to take an extra horse just in case Bart became unmanageable and had to recover from the loss of his manhood. At the last minute I decided to take the odd mule out to let Bob's dad use over winter to help pull the fish out.

And again, Noa packed our stuff on the saddled horse and threw his blankets on bare back and climbed on. Bob smiled at me. I shrugged and headed out.

We stayed at the little spring in Montana. We headed out from there the next day. The territory was covered with cattle again but no Circle C and no horses for sale. We proceeded to Bob's father's encampment on the big river. A lot of the Indians were having a tough time after the demise of the buffalo, but Bob's father found a unique source of nutrition for him and his small band. They were glad to see us.

I offered the mule to them to help pull the fish out of the river. They laughed at the mule, apparently never having ever seen such an animal before. Bob went to work demonstrating the mule's ability to pull and then saddled him and rode him around.

Bob's Father came over, unsaddled the mule, put blankets on his back, a rope Hackamore, and jumped on. The mule responded to his commands and he finally smiled. The Indians were still a proud people and still loved their horses, but the labor savings of the mule finally won them over. And besides, this was one less mouth to feed on the farm this winter.

Bob took the mule early the next morning and returned with a large buck deer. We didn't have deer around our area, so it was interesting to see one up close. After Bob skinned it, the women went to work cutting it up into strips to dry and smoke with the fish.

Bob said, "Good reprieve from eating fish three times a day."

Noa shot a grouse with my old .22 single shot rifle. After taking care of the gopher population in our pastures this summer, he was quite good with it.

"We like the grouse," he said.

We told them that we were looking for the Circle C cattle.

Bob's father immediately pointed south and said, "Across the river."

Why had I not thought to ask him before? Of course, he would know most everything that was going on around here. I gave him a thumbs up and they all laughed.

Noa said, "White man's sign language."

Everybody laughed again.

Bob demonstrated the Indian sign for understand, fingers together pointed up, palm out. I did the same thing. Got it.

I felt very comfortable staying with the Indians that night. I felt we had a mutual trust, but I was aware that didn't extend to all white people. The next morning before we left, I gave the .22 rifle and box of shells to Bob's father.

"For the grouse," I said.

He put his hands on my shoulders and said, "You are a good white man. We be friends forever."

151

"Okay," I said, giving him the palm sign and he gave me the thumbs up.

Bob was told the best crossing spot for the river, two sand bars and then to the south bank. Before too long, we saw Circle C brands. We eventually found one of the cowboys and got directions to the chuck-wagon. I could see the horses before we even got there, thirty to forty head. The cook told us where to find Harlen. He was glad to see me.

"I saved you about fifteen head," he said. "That worked out to sell you our culls and get new stock for the next drive."

Yeah, I could see they looked better and younger.

"So we gotta have a good one hundred fifty dollars a head for these."

"Okay," I said. "I might have to get a couple less. I only got two thousand dollars with me."

"Hey, did you bring that long rifle with you like you promised?"

"Yeah, I did." I called to Bob to bring it over.

"You let that Indian carry it? Is it loaded?" he asked, keeping his hand close to his revolver.

"You know some of these Indians in this country are some of the same ones that scalped old Custer and his men. That took place not too far from here."

"Yeah, I know, but I trust these two. We have the same interest in mind, horses."

After thoroughly inspecting the long rifle, he said, "I tell you what, the two thousand dollars, this rifle, and two days of rounding up steers."

I reached out to shake his hand.

He said, "I like you kid, but I got to tell you be careful out here. Over the years we've come across several dead bodies. We came across one just coming up on this last drive. Looked like he got drug to death by his horse. Not good to ride this country alone. Your horse could get spooked by anything, Indians, rustlers, a gunshot, or a rattlesnake."

"Rattlesnake, I have never seen one," I said.

"They're all over the place out here. South of here where there's nothing around and your horse throws you, you could walk for weeks and not get anywhere. Might be that the coyotes eat good. You mule farmers come out here and this is a different world."

"Okay, I understand. But you still say I'm going to have to go all the way to Texas to find a purebred quarter horse stallion?"

"Most likely," he said. "I haven't seen much else on the trail."

We went to round them up for two days and got most of the job done.

Harlen, Bob, Noa, and I cut out the horses Harlen wanted to sell me.

"Wow, those Indians do know what they're doing on horseback," he said.

"Yeah, they're hard workers. They are trying to earn enough to get a horse each," I said.

"As long as that's all they want. I never seen one I'd ever trust or hire to work for me."

He already had the rifle, so I counted out the two thousand dollars and he handed me the bill of sale.

"You coming back next year?" I asked.

"Hope to, but it's getting real crowded up here. A lot of ranches are setting up stations here again."

"Oh, didn't learn their lesson the last bad winter?" I asked.

"Apparently not, but you know a lot of these outfits are investors from back east. They don't seem to care about anything but numbers. Besides, there sure is getting to be a lot of that barbed wire around here, just like back home."

"Yeah, I noticed that too, but I suppose it was bound to happen sooner or later."

"Boy, let me tell you about back home. The wire brought out the guns, range wars we called them. Some of these guys fenced off what was once open range, so push came to shove, and the bullets started flying. Lots of people got killed. It's one of the reasons the big herds come up here. This is the last of the free range, so when it all gets fenced, that will be the end of it."

"Do you think push will come to shove here too?" I asked.

"It's hard to say, but the law enforcement is better now."

"That is an awful lot of fence."

"Texas is bigger than Montana and it's all spoken for."

"Rattlesnakes there?"

"Yeah, big ones with big teeth."

"Well Harlen, if the market holds, I'll come looking for you again next year."

"You do that kid. You know where I live," he winked, "and be careful."

We shook.

Bob and Noa were already trying out the new horses. Younger, well-trained animals were about as good a start to a good breeding herd as you could get.

I said to them, "Let's get them home so we can get to Texas."

Thumbs up and away we went. Two days later we pulled into the yard. Dad and I discussed how many we should keep given the amount of feed we had. We decided to sell half.

"Two hundred fifty dollars apiece minimum," I said.

The Canadians didn't return before we left. Dad and I only had one thousand dollars left so I reluctantly borrowed another one thousand dollars from the bank just in case I ran into a good deal. Dad would pay the loan as soon as the Canadians bought.

CHAPTER 20

Mom made fleece skin coats for Noa and Bob. They really didn't look like Indians anymore, boots, Levi jeans, and broad brimmed hats, except Noa had an eagle feather in his white domed hat.

Winter was coming on; it was starting to get cold and I was in a hurry to beat it. The Montana grouse was good.

Black Bart regained his strength. He was now reverting to his old, wild self. I still had my stick to keep him from biting. When he wanted to buck, I would spur him into a run. I would run him so hard he would be too tired to buck. Black Bart was not trained or broke. We just had a truce at times.

Our first destination was a town Harlen told me about, Milestown. Follow the south river and you can't miss it. I didn't know about the south river. Noa called it the yellow river. Evidently, he knew of it. The river didn't look yellow to me. Eventually we came to settlements and ranches.

They explained that it was the Yellowstone River and that the town we were looking for was now Miles City, named after the commanding officer at the nearby U.S. military fort.

I kept asking about horses and especially stallions for sale all along the route, but the story was always the same. Most people were trying to replenish their stock after the harsh winter losses. Sure enough, the sign said Miles City. We needed supplies, so we proceeded to the general store.

The clerk said, "There might be problems bringing those Indians in here."

"Okay," I said. "We'll get our stuff and go."

I realized we only had one gun among us. He had one new Winchester, but it was the .22 LR again.

"What are you looking for?" he asked.

"I had a Colt .45 before and that would be my first choice," I said.

"The gunsmith is just down the street and he'd be the most likely in town to have one."

"Five dollars is a lot for just a .22," I said.

"Well, it's the newer smokeless model, more power."

On a whim I said I'd take it. If Bob had it nobody could tell it wasn't the .30 caliber. It looked exactly like my .30 W.C.F. but a whole lot cheaper.

I asked the clerk the best way south out of town.

He said, "Where are you headed?"

"Texas."

He raised his eyebrows and said, "You're going through some mighty rough country down there. Pem's the guy you want to talk to. He'll be at the cantina."

"Cantina?" I repeated.

"Yeah, it's Mexican and the Indians'll be welcome there, about a half mile south of town, just this side of the river, low roofed building. Pem usually hangs out there."

I pulled Noa's feather out and pulled their hats down over their faces and we headed out. I was surprised this town had a railroad through it too.

There it was, just like the clerk described it, low building with smoke coming out of the chimney. No sign on it, but it had several horses and mules around it.

This must be the place, I thought. I gave Noa his feather back. I told them to watch the horses. If I don't come out in five minutes, come in.

It was a bar, very smoky bar. Several dark-skinned cowboys were sitting around at the tables and nobody at the bar. Dark skinned, but not Indians, I thought. Everybody looked at me like they'd never seen a white man before.

I was about to ask if Pem was here, when a voice from a dark corner table said, "What's your business stranger?"

"I'm looking for somebody," I said.

The tall skinny cowboy was sitting there with his hand out to shake, "My name's Pemberton, but everybody calls me Pem."

"Call me Bill," I said, shaking his hand.

"Well, sit down, wet your throat, and state your business."

Pem had a bottle of whiskey in front of him and a cigarette in one hand.

"I don't drink whiskey much," I said, "but I could use some water."

That brought a good laugh to the whole place.

Pem was an older man and wore a large cowboy hat with a feather in it.

"I'm on my way to Texas to buy horses and was wondering which was the best way to go."

Pem laughed, "You're pretty young and you never been there before, have you?"

"No, you're right."

"Well, you're heading to the right place for good horse stock. I'm from Texas, came up with the drives and liked the place, the open range. I got me a little place down the river, so little that the big outfits don't fool with me. Got some frontage. That's where the buildings are, twenty head of horses and one hundred to one hundred fifty cattle. No use trying to get any bigger. The big boys would try to squeeze me out. I've kept it all these years and I use Mexicans for hands, so nobody bothers me, Most people know I was pretty good with a gun back in my driver days."

"Still a lot of gun play around here?" I asked.

"Not so much anymore, just the drunk cowboys on Saturday night shooting up the town. But we got a sheriff and lots of deputies now. So the cowboys find themselves in jail."

Pem went on and gave me the whole history of the Miles City area and the ranching there. I asked him about buying horses around there.

"Don't think so," he said. "The cattle business goes through them as fast as they can buy or breed them. No, I'd say you'd have to go all the way to Texas all right."

"What's the best route?" I asked.

"You by yourself?" he asked.

"No, I got two hands outside," I said.

"Well, bring 'em in."

"They're Indians."

"Well, these are mostly Mexicans in here and if you're going to Texas, that's mostly what's down there."

"Any good quarter stallions down there?"

"I'm sure there is," he said. "That's big horse country."

"No place closer?"

"My guess is probably not, but you could check on the way. If you go straight south, you'll be in some dry, sparce country inhabited by Indians. If you veer east, it'll be easier going, more settlers, safer, but probably not many horses for sale. But now if you're sure with your guns and got partners with their guns, you could veer west and skirt the mountains."

"Yeah, that's the way I want to go," I said. "I have never seen the mountains but have heard and read a lot about them. Are they really as big as they say?"

"I say they are, and you'd see the biggest going the west route. You'd be in ranch country and more likely to come across horses for sale or you might even come across some wild mustangs to chase down."

Pem really had my interest now, "Wild mustangs, are there any still around?"

"The low land ones are pretty scarce. You'd be lucky to find some. But I've heard in the high plateau country down there starting by Laramie, there are thousands of them. Nobody can catch them. They have big lungs from living in the high mountains and because of that they can run for long distances."

Right away I thought of Bart and wondered if he could stand a chance of outracing mustangs.

"Laramie?" I asked.

"Yeah, head southwest out of here. You'll follow the Yellowstone until you get to Rosebud. Follow it and keep due south until you see some mountains. That'll be the Big Horns. Skirt along on the east side of them and head due south. You'll cross a big valley but keep those far-off south mountains in sight. They're the start of the plateau country. Laramie will be in the foothills there somewhere.

You'll run into lots of ranches and a few Indians. I figure there's got to be a few towns down there since I last rode it. It's kind of funny you know, all these railroads go east and west, but there doesn't seem to be any that go north and south."

"Yeah, I never thought about that," I said. "How's a guy supposed to go down there except on horseback?"

I brought the Indians in there and we ate. I bought Pem a meal and he let us stay at his place. He had two bunk houses there.

I got to thinking about Pem's remarks about the guns, so I went back to the gun shop.

"What are you looking for?" the clerk asked.

"I had a Colt .45 before."

He showed me a whole bunch of used ones he reworked but didn't seem to have any new ones.

"If you're going south, you better have a .45 minimum," he said.

"My other guns are the smokeless power," I said.

He appeared deep in thought and then went to the back room.

He came back with a wooden box, which had a shiny new Colt .45 in it. The barrel was longer, but it had the black finish and nice wooden handles. It felt great. I was sold. The tag said seven dollars and fifty cents.

"I really didn't want to sell this one, but I ordered two more. So, if you really need it, I could let you have it for ten dollars."

"It says seven dollars and fifty cents on it."

"You won't find another around here like this. It's built stronger for the smokeless powder."

"Yeah, I know."

"Ten dollars and I'll throw in a box of smoke-less ammo."

"Okay, and I'll buy another box."

"Okay, now let's look at holsters."

"Woah," I said. "This is enough. Maybe next time. I'm spent out."

"You got gun oil for it?"

"Yes, I do."

I handed him the money and left. Wow, ten dollars, but it was exactly what I wanted.

CHAPTER 21

The next morning Pem's wife was making breakfast when I came in. He handed me a cup of coffee and offered a chair.

"I sure appreciate all the advice you've given me. Nice place you got here."

"Better here than Texas. The range wars got too hot for me down there," he said. "But the same's happening up here, except they're not using bullets."

"No bullets? How are they driving the little guys out?" I asked.

"Bankrupting them," he returned.

"Bankrupting," I repeated.

"Yeah, messing up their herds somehow, stealing the calves before they're branded, hiring rustlers, or stampeding their herds during bad weather. But their latest tactics are fire. The last two range fires we had around here were just at the right place and the wind just right, so it wipes out some of the smaller outfits. They couldn't pay their hands, so they went to work for the big outfits."

"And all without a shot fired," I said.

"You got it. My Mexican men are loyal to me. I treat them right, so they stick around. We only had one fire come through here, but luckily, we saw it coming and got all the stock into the river so they couldn't stampede, and it kept them out of the fire. And so far since then nothing has happened."

"So you think these bigger outfits would resort to rustling?" I asked.

"Well, in Texas we called them mavericks, animals with no marking on them out running the range, so their possession is ten-tenths of the law. Any disputes are handled with guns. Say boy, what is your brand anyway?"

"Well, I don't have one. I just use my dad's."

"You better think about getting one. When you're driving stock down here you better either have them branded or papers for them."

"But if they're not marked, then ten-tenths of the law come into effect, right?" I asked.

"Yeah, if you can keep possession of them, that's when lots of fire power comes into effect."

I hadn't expected this. The dime novels were becoming a little more realistic.

"You know I wouldn't mind getting a pure quarter stallion either," he said. "Mine used to be mostly quarters, but over the years they've been bred to whatever's around. So, if you find an extra one, bring him back. You can stay here anytime. I don't know if I'll ever get down there again, so stop in every time you're nearby. I'd love to hear the latest from down that way."

"Okay, thanks. We'll be back through here unless we're on a wild horse chase somewhere."

We shook and off we went. Following the rivers southwest, we were in view of the mountains in two days. There were several small ranches on the way.

We stayed at a couple houses. They all had the same story, tough going living amongst the large herds.

The Big Horns were getting bigger every day. I was amazed by their size. I had never seen anything like it. Looking up to the peaks, I wondered if there were any wild horses running around up there. What else was up there? I had to wonder.

Before we got to the foothills, we started to encounter Indian bands, lots of them. Some of them had horses, some had cattle, and one band even had sheep. I was surprised. Bob and Noa were not overly concerned about them at all, and we passed through uneventfully.

Eventually, we came to Big Horn, Wyoming. Mounted up on the livery stable were the biggest set of funny deer antlers I ever saw.

"Wapiti," Noa said.

I looked at Bob.

"Very big deer," Bob shrugged.

Noa spoke again, then Bob said, "Bear also." He pointed to the mountains.

After having read my dime novels, I knew what a bear was but had never seen one of those either. I was hoping we could see them all. Bears, giant deer, and rattlesnakes, what else could there be?

I was surprised at how nice the town was and how many businesses there were out here in the wilderness. Then I found out why. There was a train through here also.

Bob and Noa seemed to be accepted here. I started to see why there were Indians everywhere here. They were not a novelty, and nobody paid any attention to them.

Bob and Noa seemed at ease here and they were accepted in the general store where we got resup-plied. I was amazed at what was available in the store that seemed to be way out here in the wilderness.

"That's what a train will bring you," the clerk said. "The prices are lower."

"Yeah, but half of us lost our stagecoach jobs," an old timer sitting in the corner said.

Progress, I thought. It's coming along with the settlers. Pemberton was right. South of Big Horn, we ran into sparse country, sparse grass and even less water, but we could see the beginnings of the next set of mountains far to the south of us. And that's where Laramie was supposed to be.

I wondered how friendly the people would be down there. It looked like we'd be crossing a broad plain valley and there were bound to be large ranches here. Hopefully, we could pass through unscathed. We rode hard, walking the horses at night and trying to sleep in the saddle.

Noa said, "The horses need little sleep if we keep them safe. If they don't get spooked at night by predators, they could rest well and put in a long day and part of the night."

So, we kept them close at camp and I could hear Noa talking to them. We came to only one ranch across there and they were friendly enough. We bought a meal there and slept in their barn.

In the morning they told us to head due south through the foothills until we intersected the stage road between Casper and Laramie, turn left and head south. Eventually you would get to Laramie.

"Thanks," I said.

The grass got better as we got into the foothills and the cattle got thicker. We saw three different brands. Two horses stood in a tall grass meadow, so we meandered on over there. I thought I could see remnants of an old brand and slight bridle mark. I figured them as older horses because they looked heavy and not worked recently.

"Must belong to somebody," I said. Looked like old brands, so we kept going.

We hadn't gone a hundred yards before I heard them, horses coming hard. For some reason I felt uneasy about it. Sure enough, two cowboys, guns drawn.

"You boys looking to steal those horses?"

"No, does it look like it?"

"You came up on 'em and looked at them."

"Yeah, and then we moved on."

They looked at each other. One said, "Those are Indians. I never seen an Indian with as good a horse as that unless he stole it."

"Those are my horses and these gentlemen work for me."

"You got any proof those are your horses?" he asked.

"Yes, I do."

They were studying the Indians. Seeing us unarmed except our rifles, they dropped their gun barrels.

I stabbed my hand into my saddle bag and brought out my new .45 and pointed it directly at his chest.

"You even twitch those guns and you're a goner and I think I can get you too," I told the other.

They looked at each other and said, "Okay."

"Now drop them right down on the ground there."

They looked at each other again, as if one of them should know what to do.

I said, "You can either drop them or I can shoot them out of your hands. I been shooting gophers all my life and those guns are about the same size. I haven't missed one in the last two years."

The closest one could tell he'd be the first to get it, so he let it drop.

I pointed at the other cowboy and said, "I guess I gotta shoot you first now."

He leaned over and with two fingers as gently as he could, let it drop.

"Now, keep your hands out there where I can see them so I can figure out how to load this thing."

Before they could react, I had two rounds in it. They looked at each other like, did this guy just take us with an empty gun?

"Come on Harley, let's take him. He can't shoot us without getting hung."

"Yeah," Harley said.

I said, "Now that you're the first one in line, go for it."

"If something happens here, we're in the right," the first Cowboy said. "We'll testify you tried to steal our horses."

"Three against two," I said.

"Yeah, but you got two Indians."

"Yeah, but you got nobody. You forgot dead men tell no tales."

Harley looked at the first cowboy like what do we do now?

I reached the gun out to them just about equidistant between their two horses heads and asked, "How does this thing work anyway?"

I pulled the hammer back to just before cock and let it go. The ensuing explosion sent their horses into rodeo mode and Bart not far behind.

I knew the Texas horses were gun trained. Bart was not, but I knew how to spur him into a run when he wanted to buck and away we went.

Noa and Bob knew what was up and were in front of me. We were diverging away from each other.

Good, I thought. If the bullets started flying there'd be too many targets.

When I was sure there was a clear path in front of Bart, I looked back and saw they were still fighting with their horses. We were quickly getting out of range, over and around the hill, out of sight. I slowed to a trot. Noa and Bob ended up well behind me.

"Wow," they said, "Bart was moving."

"Yeah, he was."

I had run him before but not like that. It didn't take much to spur him into a run, but I spurred him hard that time and he responded.

"He would make a good Indian pony," Noa said. I could tell he was impressed and that was saying something because Noa must have seen a lot of horses in his day.

We kept an eye out behind us. Nobody followed. I hoped none of those cowboys had been hurt in our little incident, but they were the ones that had brought it on, even though it was obvious we had ridden by those horses.

I got to thinking, I bet they put those old horses there as a trap to try to catch rustlers. Not a bad idea, but it was pretty obvious we had ridden on. So why the harassment? We better watch ourselves here, I thought. That was the first time I shot the new .45.

"Maybe we should take some time and do a little target practice," I said.

Noa pointed off to the left, more prairie dogs. Perfect, I thought.

Bob said, "If you can hit a prairie dog, you can hit anything."

When we got there, there were dog holes for as far as you could see in that direction. There was no end to the targets.

I tried to teach Bob windage and elevation. The farther the target was away, the higher you had to aim. If you were shooting extremely close, you had to aim low.

We tried targets at all ranges. Our shooting was improving, so I was glad we stopped there. Bob was really enjoying it.

"I'll get all the grouse now," he said.

Just then Noa started talking and gesturing, "Rider coming."

"Keep your gun barrels down all the time," I told Bob.

A single cowboy came at a slow run, no gun out. He rode up and said, "Howdy."

"Howdy," I said.

"I just came over here to see what all the shooting was about?"

"Oh, we're just target practicing on the dogs," I said.

He seemed very friendly. Sam was his name. We shook and I told him mine.

His demeanor changed when he saw two of us were Indian.

Before he could say anything, I told him we were from Montana and were on our way to Texas to buy horses.

"Seems like a long way to go just to buy horses," he said.

I told him about buying the quarter mares from the drivers, but that they never had any pure quarter stallions. Then I asked him if there was anything like that around here. I got cash money.

"Well, you're sitting on one," he said.

"I know, but so far no colts."

"I see. Well none that I can think of. We're kind of in the same boat around here."

He must have started believing my story because he got friendlier.

"Are we going the right direction to intercept the Laramie Road?" I asked.

"About thirty or forty miles, then left. First ranch should be the Shilo Ranch. Jesse and Slim are nice guys. They cater to the coach people, so it's a good place to eat."

"Just what we're looking for," I said. "Thanks."

We headed for the road, a little more confident of our shooting abilities.

You never know what kind of people you could run into out here; some are friendly, and some want to arrest you for horse thieving just for looking at the horse.

We finally came to a brook running northwest by southeast. I could see a road across on the other slope. We were watering the horses in the bottom when a coach rumbled by.

"Must be the right place," Bob said.

"Yeah."

We didn't go two miles down the road and there it was, the Shilo Ranch. We knew because it was painted on the large barn. I couldn't think of any ranch I had ever been to that had the name painted in large letters on the barn.

As we got closer, two men approached us. I told them who I was and that we were passing through and were wondering if we could buy some food.

"Yeah, I'm Slim. This is Jesse. Come on in. We feed the coach passengers and I think we have some grub on the stove."

Not knowing what they thought about the Indians, I said we could eat out here. But they insisted on us coming in. They didn't seem to mind the Indians at all. They had a large table where they feed the coach riders. The beef stew was very good after eating on the trail. They had a lady cooking for them that was in her mid 50s. She made great apple pie, which I didn't think I would find out here.

Jesse asked where we were headed. I told him going to Texas hopefully to buy some quarter horses and a quarter stallion, unless I could find some closer to here.

"This whole state is full of cattle and every horse is in use. You're right in going to Texas. That's where the horse ranches are. We're in constant need of horses ourselves," Jesse said.

"We run a stagecoach weigh station here to supplement the ranch. To keep the stage line going, it takes a lot of horses."

"We're from up Montana way and the settlers are coming in, so they all need horses also," I said, "so I am trying to work up a breeding herd. You ever tried to breed any horses here?"

"We try," he said, "but it takes time and good breeding stock, so it's a challenge. You all from Montana? I've wanted to go to Montana for a long time. I've heard so much about it. You've also got me thinking about going to Texas with you."

"Well, the more the better," I said.

"Your idea of getting a superior blood line is a good idea. The stage line is always buying good horses and we could use some better horses around here too."

"Wow," I said. "Sounds like the whole country could be in the market for horses."

"Yeah," Jesse said. "I'd say so."

"I've heard of wild horses in the mountains down here somewhere."

Jesse got a big smile on his face and said, "If you're talking about the mountain mustangs you heard right. Most all the wild horses on the plains or wherever that are easy to catch have been taken. The mountain mustangs are there because nobody can catch them. And believe me many have tried."

Noa spoke and gestured and pointed. We both looked at Bob.

"He says your black horse is very fast and can catch the mustangs."

Jesse chuckled, "I can guarantee you a whole lot of people thought that. We went up there with twenty men one time and some of the fastest horses around here. We came back completely wore out and not one mustang to show for it. There's a lot of high country up there for them. The only thing that drives them down is the snow."

"We actually caught a couple one time when the snow was so bad that they come all the way down to our haystacks and we caught two older ones. Even those old ones were fantastic horses. They're living up in the mountains and the thin air causes them to have larger lungs. Climbing around in the mountains all the time causes them to have more muscle so they can outrun most any other horse."

I realized I was sitting on the edge of my seat, listening to Jesse. He noticed it too.

"Looks like you boys would be up for giving them a chase."

I noticed Bob and Noa on the edge of their seats also, intently listening.

"Most fantastic thing I ever heard of myself," I said. I wondered about the wild horses, mountains, giant deer, bears, and all the trees.

"We have to drive a wagon forty miles to buy lumber off the train and then drive back home. I'd really like to see that high country even if we don't have a chance for the mustangs."

"Let's go and catch the Indian ponies," Noa said.

Bob had his usual big smile on his face.

CHAPTER 22

"Well, it all depends on the snow," Jesse said. "There's too much area to find them in the summer months. But there's snow up there now, so we could go up there and look around."

"You would go with us?" I asked.

"I'm always ready to go up into the mountains," he said, "depending on the workload here. We have a few haying odds and ends to finish up here and then I could go."

We were so excited, we pitched in to help. Noa and Bob became experts at rehitching the new teams to the stage. Slim said we earned more than our room and board.

Jesse said we had to prepare for the trip. "You don't just go riding up into the mountains without having everything planned." But he did say we looked like we had the right gear for it, fleece lined coats and fleece lined bed rolls.

"I wish I had something like that," he said.

"I'll get you some," I said.

"I know they're the best," he said, "but the way sheep are looked down upon around here, I never got around to getting any."

"The big cattle outfits running rough shod around here, too?" I asked.

"Yeah, absentee owners with money to hire all the hands and that's what it takes to rule."

"Yeah, some back home," I said.

"We got this little corner up here, so small nobody bothers us. If we didn't have the stagecoach contract, we wouldn't be around."

"Let's hope the train doesn't come through here anytime soon," I said.

"Slim already thought about that and suggested we'd put in a coal station for the train."

I laughed, "Would you rather shovel coal or wrangle horses for a living?"

"You don't even have to ask that," Jesse said.

After all the work was done, we got our horses packed. The Shilo Ranch lay high in the foothills, so we were in the mountains as soon as we left the ranch.

Jesse took his best horse and raced me out of the yard just to see how fast my black stallion was, and he was impressed. I spurred Bart hard and he outdistanced Jesse's best by a long distance. But Bart got winded in a shorter distance than usual, so I was beginning to understand the thinner air of the high mountains. We waited, resting our horses for Bob and Noa to catch up with the pack horses. Jesse carried a large rifle, "The kind to hunt elk," he said.

"Elk are larger than deer and more skittish. It is hard to get very close to them, so you have to use an old buffalo gun to hunt them."

The Sharps was so big it wouldn't fit in a scabbard, so Jesse carried it across his saddle.

I asked him if anybody ever lived up here.

"Only a few prospectors back when," he said. "The snow gets too deep to stay up here over winter, so you couldn't live there long. We'll have to go all the way up to the snow elevation. The mustangs have to come down out of the snow to find grass to find anything to eat."

The cold was even worse because of the wind. We camped in the trees to try to stay out of it. We could see the snow level up there as we went along. I couldn't believe the view. Nobody back home would believe it. Always climbing and with the added burden of the thin air, it seemed like it took us a long time, but we finally got there.

Jesse led us into the trees just before we crossed the last bluff. We dismounted and walked the rest of the way. I was breathing hard and felt funny. Jesse and Noa laughed at Bob and I, like they knew something that we didn't.

Over the bluff and down to the edge of the trees, there they were. Jesse knew where to find them. I had never seen so many horses in one area before. Big, magnificent horses of all colors, all grazing peacefully over the valley. It seemed as if we could ride right out there and herd them all home. I was in a state of euphoria and I could tell Bob was mesmerized.

"What do we do now?" I asked Jesse.

He laughed and said, "You tell me."

Bob said, "I will get our horses."

He came back to just inside the trees. We mounted up and decided to come out of the trees at a dead run, so we could get on them before they had a chance to run. I spurred Black Bart like never before. He put his head down and gave it his all. I figured it was the fastest I'd ever been on a horse.

There was a loud whinnie from up above and the mustangs took off. I don't know if it was farther than it seemed, but the slowest of them came from below, passed us, and ran up the mountain before we got a third of the way across the valley. It was like we were trying to outrace the wind and I somehow felt high or euphoric.

It was amazing to watch those horses run like that in these conditions. I felt like I was riding a lightning bolt. As the horses went up the mountain, I turned Bart up also, but he soon slowed to a trot and then a walk. He was blowing hard. He was completely winded.

I got off and loosened the saddle. I noticed Bob had done the same thing quite a ways back. I tried to lead him around, but he didn't move. Bart probably couldn't believe those horses had done that to him. He wanted to run with them and had overdone it.

I unsaddled him and got some grass and rubbed him down. He had a hard time recovering in this thin air, but I finally laid the saddle on him and led him back to Jesse and Noa, who were laughing.

"How many did you catch?" they asked, laughing again.

Bob looked at me and shrugged.

"Yeah, I see the problem now," I said. "This is going to be a tough one."

"If these mustangs were any easier to catch, they probably wouldn't be here," Jesse said.

"Yeah," I said, "but if you ever caught one, you would have a hell of a horse."

Noa pointed back up the mountain valley and there stood a large speckled gray mustang stallion. It was hard to tell the size from this distance, but I could tell that was a large horse.

"I'll bet that's the big lead stallion," Jesse said. "Old timers around here say the only way you'll ever catch any of these wild mountain horses is by shooting the stallion. It would disorganize them enough that you could cut some of them off and chase them down the valley that leads down to our ranch. If we could ever cut some of them off and get them into that draw, we could herd them right down to our corrals. But you can't cut them off from above because they stay right at the snow line, so there is always snow above them. No rider can get into that deep snow to cut them off and chase them down."

That big stallion reared up on his hind legs and disappeared. Wow, shoot a horse like that? I wondered if I could ever pull the trigger on such a beautiful animal.

I turned to Noa and Bob and asked, "How do we catch them?"

"Indians can't catch them either," Noa said.

"We'll have to leave and let them settle down and come back to the snow line," Jesse said. So, we reluctantly headed back down the mountain, my mind completely abuzz as to how to get those horses.

Since we were up there, Jesse was wanting to hunt elk. He led us to a different area of the mountain that he thought would most likely have elk on it. What I took as a strong cow track turned out to be elk tracks. We tracked them until Noa said they were just in front of us in the trees. So, Jesse and I proceeded on foot leaving the horses with Bob and Noa.

I told Jesse about the new .30 caliber smokeless rifle. He seemed less than impressed.

"Remember, these aren't deer. They're much bigger and need a lot more power to bring down."

We walked to within two hundred yards of them. We worked our way around to be downwind.

Jesse looked around for the perfect tree to hide behind. It had a branch at just the right height to rest the heavy Sharps on. We waited for most of a half hour before a large bull emerged on our side of the herd. Before I could get a look at him, the big Sharps went off. The bull hunched.

"Shoot!" Jesse yelled.

I got off two shots before they were gone. We whistled at Bob and Noa to bring the horses. There was a lot of blood where the bull was hit, so he was easy to trail. After a quarter mile we found him dead, laying in the snow. All the others were gone, so my feeble attempt with the .30 WCF was all for not.

I was impressed, the biggest deer like animal I had ever seen. Bob and Noa had smiles on their faces, meat, and lots of it.

CHAPTER 23

We returned to Shilo Ranch. Bob and Noa got busy cutting and smoking the meat. We would have plenty of grub for our trip to Texas. Jesse said it would take another snow to drive the mustangs back down far enough for us to get another chance at them.

"You're still planning on going to Texas?" he asked.

"Yeah, " I answered, "unless I could find some good quarter horse studs closer."

"Likely not," he said. "Besides, we need to let those mustangs calm down and start moving down the mountain."

"Yeah, so we'll head south in a day or two if the weather holds. It shouldn't take us more than a month, should it?" I asked.

"Just to ride down there and back wouldn't take half that long," he replied, "but to get what you're looking for could add another couple of weeks. You're riding into different country down there. All big cattle ranches come about and were built with spilt blood. Probably a lot of the livestock were acquired the same way."

"No homesteading down there?" I asked.

"Not much," he said. "You don't get two hundred thousand acres by homesteading it. The toughest man takes all. So make sure you have a copy of your brand for your horses and get a good bill of sale for anything you acquire."

"Okay," I said. "You almost scared me out of it."

"I just want to let you know how it is down there. Back when that blood was spilled for those ranches, there wasn't hardly any law down there. There's not a whole lot more now. They're spread pretty thin because the country is too big. And to add to that, there are renegade Indians that love horses as much as your boys there."

"Okay," I said.

Slim gave me a detailed map of the best route to Texas horse country and the same advice Jesse had given us.

After helping around the ranch, we headed south the next day, keeping in mind what they told me. We kept away from the bigger towns and tried to stay out of sight as much as possible. For the most part Colorado was pretty settled until we got to the southeast corner. The land became sandier and the forage sparce. People were even more sparce.

When we finally got to Oklahoma, we were in a different world, a few cows here and there. We came to a small town. The people seemed to stand around and stare at us as if we were the strangest thing they had ever seen, especially when they saw two Indians dressed as cowboys.

I asked one of them if there was a place we could get some food and supplies. They didn't talk, they just pointed to a nondescript building with no sign on it. I went in and asked if I could get some food and supplies.

"What do you want?" he asked.

"Anything you got to eat," I said.

199

"Beef and beans on a tortilla?" he asked.

"Great, give me three of them."

Just then one of the men in there came up behind me and asked what I was doing around these parts?

I turned to see who it was and saw a big star on a big man. The star said Deputy on it. He didn't have a smile on his face or offer to shake hands. So, I started to tell him I was from Montana and headed to Texas to try and find a quarter stud horse.

"You got money to buy horses?" he asked.

"Well yeah, a little," I said, "hopefully enough to buy a good stud horse."

"Yeah, well 99% of the varmints that come around here are either outlaws or renegade Indians," he nodded towards the door as if he knew who I was with, "coming in to steal whatever they can find."

"Oh, not me sir. I'm only here to buy. You see I have Texas quarter horses at my place in Montana and need a stud horse to start my own herd of pure-breds. I've been told the only place to get one is at one of the horse ranches in Texas, unless somebody around here could tell me where I could get one closer around here."

"How come you're here with a couple of Indians?" he asked.

"They're with me. I'll vouch for them. They're the best horse wranglers and trainers I could find to come with me."

His facial expression changed as if he was starting to believe me.

"Well, you don't talk like you're from around here, so you must be a Yankee or something. And you heard right, it's hard to come by good horse flesh around here. Texas is the place to go for that. But tell me, say you go and find some really good horses. You going to try and get them all the way through this outlaw and Indian country back to Montana? That's straight up the outlaw trail and I can assure you outlaws and Indians are always on the lookout for good horses."

I thought fast and said that I had a good friend in Texas by the name of Harlen, who works for the Circle C, and drove cattle up to Montana every spring to get them fattened for market. We plan to hook up with them and wrangle cattle there and bring the horses with us.

"Oh well, you might make it then," he said. "Good luck boys and don't take any wooden nickels." He laughed and walked away.

We looked at each other and mouthed "wooden nickels."

The southern food was great. It had something to do with the spices.

The next town we came to was Amarillo, Texas. I was surprised that only five days after leaving Shilo Ranch, we were in Texas. Noa was right. With proper feed and rest, the horses could go with little sleep, but that made for many fourteen to sixteen hour days, mostly in the saddle.

The information we got in Amarillo was that the bigger horse ranches were in southern Texas. As we proceeded south, the country got hotter and drier, even though it was in the middle of winter back home in Dakota. I wondered what it was like down here in the middle of summer.

I could see why they drove the cattle up north from here. The forage was pretty sparse. It was definitely all ranch country. No farming here, only garden plots wherever people lived.

For the most part most of the people here looked like they lived a pretty sparce existence and were wary of strangers, especially Indian strangers. So, we took to having Noa and Bob stay in camp while I went into town for supplies and information. Apparently, a lot of the people around here were old enough to remember the Indian Wars and were not friendly at all.

We were eventually directed to a place called Eldorado, where there were supposed to be some bigger horse ranches. As we proceeded south, the land got hotter, drier, and more sparce. The people were darker skinned and less friendly. More and more of them were wearing revolvers and rifles on their saddles.

I was thoroughly amazed that it could be so hot and dry here, while it was the middle of winter back in Dakota. I couldn't help but wonder how cold it was. It had been twenty degrees to thirty degrees below zero back there this time of year. I was definitely in a different land. But I was excited as were Noa and

Bob. We were going to hopefully purchase some of the best horses anybody back home had ever seen.

CHAPTER 24

Three riders appeared to our right. When they saw us, they altered their direction toward us.

I said, "Just keep heading south."

But they soon rode up next to us, three of the toughest looking cowboys I'd ever seen, wearing those leather chaps I'd heard about. Lots of guns and covered with dust. They were riding their big, beautiful, gelded quarter horses.

"Indians," one of them said in a very non-friendly tone.

"Howdy," I said, waving.

"Well, howdy yourself greenhorn," the first cowboy returned menacingly.

"Wow, look at those shiny new guns he's got," the third one said, pointing at my new Colt .45.

"Yeah," I said, "the new smokeless powder .45, about three times more powerful than the old black power."

"You don't say," the first one said, whipping out his revolver and putting a three inch hole into a strange looking round plant about the size of a pumpkin with sharp spines on it. I knew what he was up to, so I was about a second behind him. The smokeless .45 blew the round green plant completely away. Small pieces of it came floating back to earth. The first two cowboys looked on in complete amazement.

The third one said, "Wow, we got to get us some of these boys."

"What you boys up to?" the first one asked.

"We're down here from up north looking to purchase some of those fine Texas horses like you boys are sitting on."

"That's a pretty nice black stud you got there," one said.

"You got money to buy horses?"

Thinking fast I said, "Well no, we got a friend down here, Harlen from the Circle C. He owes us for wrangling and we wanted to get some good horses for the drive back north."

The macho went away when they heard that name and hopefully any trouble.

The third one asked if that shiny new lever action was smokeless also.

"Yes," I said, whipping it out.

"How about a demo shot?" he asked.

"Well, I would, but a dollar a trigger pull," I lied. "Fast, straight, and long distance. A dollar is the bad news, but the good news is that it only takes one trigger pull."

They looked on in dead silence not knowing what to say.

"You guys work the ranches around here? You know where we could get some good horse flesh?"

"Yeah," one of them said. "Cut south and a little east," pointing. "The Triple M is one of the bigger horse places around, about ten to twenty miles I'd say."

"Thanks, I appreciate the info," I said.

"Yeah, well you Yankee and Indians have a good day," one of them said as they turned to ride off.

"Yeah, you too," I returned and waved. Amazingly they waved back.

"Wow, that could have been trouble," Bob said.

"Yeah, good shootin," Noa said.

"Yeah, tough is the name of the game," I said. "I guess the penny dreadfuls were right about the wild west. Their leather chaps looked heavy and hot."

"Yeah, but they protect you from the cactus," Noa said.

"Yeah, everything down here seems to have long, sharp needles on them," I said.

"What were those extra loops on the saddles for?" Bob asked.

"Their whips," I said. "Apparently the southern cattle are so wild they need whips to keep them in line."

"You still got some of those penny dreadfuls with you?" Bob asked.

"Yeah," I said, handing him one.

"I don't know how to read very good yet," he said.

"Start reading aloud and I'll help you," I said.

Bob started reading and I corrected him when he got to a word he didn't know. Eventually Bob got to reading better and better. I noticed Noa riding closer and listening. He obviously liked the story.

Before we knew it, we got to a fence that stretched each way for as far as we could see, which headed down to lower country and possibly water. We followed it.

We finally reached a trail going through the fence and a big gate. Sticks were arranged to form three Ms, but no building or people in sight. We proceeded through and followed the trail. We were soon intercepted by two cowboys, who wanted to know our business there. By their tone I could tell they thought we were up to no good, probably the sight of the Indians.

I said, "We're looking for horses and want to speak to the owner."

They looked at each other and finally decided to take us in. McAllen was the boss' name. There had been three of them, but Richard McAllen and his son were the only ones left.

"What happened?" I asked.

"Trouble," was their only reply.

They didn't talk much, just rode on. After several miles we got to a green, broad area of the stream next to some low hills. There was a large ranch house, some out buildings and corrals. A few horses and cattle were grazing around.

As we got closer, a Mexican kid ran to the house and yelled, "Mr. McAllen, some riders."

After a few minutes, a bigger, older man came to the door. He looked a little put out for the interruption. Without a smile, he waved me in.

"What is it you want, boy?" he said in a gruff voice.

I told him my story and told him I needed some good quarter horse studs.

With a wrinkle in his brow he asked, "You got money, boy?"

I thought it's time to show my hand, otherwise this guy was going to throw me out. I pulled off my money belt and whipped out my cash.

He studied it for a second and then put out his hand and with a smile said, "Richard McAllen."

He led the way in. He sat in a large leather stuffed chair and pointed at a decanter on the mantle and two glasses.

"Pour 'em, would you? I'm not a good host. Too many years in the saddle I guess and now it's too much time in this damn chair. But my boy Adam should be able to take over. He runs into trouble now and again, so I have to get out and straighten things up. My brothers and I started almost 50 years ago here."

He proceeded to tell me his whole life story about the ranch.

"But good men and more importantly good horses are what you need in this country."

Then he told me the whole lineage of the Texas quarter horse.

"That's why I'm here sir," I said. "I know these are the best horses in the country."

He yelled at the Mexican boy to go fetch Fernando. We continued talking and finally Fernando, a smaller Mexican came running in. McAllen asked him if all the stallions at the south place had been gelded yet.

"I don't think so but could look."

"Go and get some better ones and bring them back for this gentleman to look at, would you?"

"Would you take my partners with?" I asked.

"Okay," Fernando said, "running out the door."

"How far north are you?" McAllen asked.

"Montana Dakota area," I answered.

212

"Wow, you are a long way from home."

"Yeah, but this is as far as I had to go to get top quality horses," I said.

"Montana, always wanted to see Montana. A lot of outfits around here run cattle up there. I would have loved to do that, but it takes a lot of good men. A tough job, only for young men," he said pouring from the decanter.

I sipped slowly as I was not used to too much liquor. Besides there was the old rumor that these big ranchers used liquor to make the bargaining go smoother. We talked for most of an hour, mostly him wanting to hear about the north country.

Eventually Bob, Noa, and Fernando returned with the quarter horse studs. Bob and Noa had big smiles on their faces, so I knew they liked the horses. Five in all, three older ones and a couple of two year olds. The younger horses were good looking and just exactly what I was looking for, one paint and one chestnut. As I was looking them over, Mr. McAllen gave me the whole story and how closely they were related to some of the original Texas quarter horses.

Every time I looked at Bob and Noa, they seemed very excited, which got me excited. We had gone through a lot to get to this point and here they were, so I need to put on my best poker face.

Finally, I said, "How much?"

"Six hundred a piece or one thousand for both."

He didn't mention any price for the older studs. So much for my poker face. He knew what I wanted and how bad. Bob and Noa's big smiles didn't help.

"Well, that's a lot more than I wanted to spend," I said, thinking that's probably all I could get for them in Canada even after I got them home.

"Good young horses, a good blood line as you will find anywhere," he said, "lots of years of service."

He was right and it didn't help that Bob and Noa just kept on smiling.

"That's your best price?" I asked.

"Yeah," he said. "We normally don't sell studs because that's our trade. We usually only sell work horses to keep the market from getting saturated," he said.

"Besides, I like you, kid and you live far enough away, probably wouldn't affect the Texas market anyway."

Wow, he had me. He had been in the horse business a long time and knew how to sell them. He wasn't a success by accident. He was good and I had to learn from his expertise.

Noa didn't usually have much expression on his face, but his head was imperceptibly shaking yes. I walked up the step and pointed into the house while removing my money belt.

Mr. McAllen wrote out a perfect bill of sale, the exact color, description of the horses, and the brand. He invited us to stay and eat beef, beer, and tortillas.

The next morning, we headed south to another ranch to see what else we could find. Fernando sent us there.

"Some of my family," he said.

We picked up four unrelated broodmares there, two year olds also. No studs for sale.

After spending two thousand dollars, I was ready to head north.

I left Bob and Noa out of town while I went in to get supplies.

I tethered the horses in front of the Sonora Trade Goods Emporium and went in.

I heard some excited talk about a man by the name of El Concho. I didn't know what it was about, so I got my stuff and left. We bought two old five dollar saddles from the ranches, so I proceeded to tie our supplies to them. Before I got done a very overweight, dark Mexican came walking down the street, a whiskey bottle in one hand and a revolver in the other. I hoped he would walk by, but he didn't.

He stopped and said, "You have fine horses. I want to buy one."

"Sorry, these are not for sale. You might find one down at the livery for sale."

"Oh, not as good as these," he said. "I have money."

I looked at him for the first time. He put a dirty hand into his pocket and pulled out a wad of dirty bills of some kind and held them up in the air.

"No thanks," I said. "I got these for my ranch. I don't want to sell."

He fired his revolver into the air and said, "Maybe I'll just take one!" then laughed.

He was unsteady on his feet and had a hard time focusing his eyes, obviously drunk and maybe dangerous. Somebody nearby whispered at me, El Concho. Oh great, that must mean trouble. I wanted to whisper back doesn't this town have a sheriff, but the man was gone.

El Concho laughed again and said, "Maybe I'll just shoot one, then you will have one less anyway."

I was wondering how I could get out of this when a shot rang out. The horses reared and jumped and almost pulled loose from their tie up. Then I saw one of them had a bloody bullet nick on the back of his leg.

I lost my head and ran out into the street. El Concho was lowering his bottle from a long drink when he saw me. He immediately started drawing his gun. I was in shock. Was this really happening? Time seemed to slow down.

El Concho seemed to sober up. His eyes were focused, and he was raising that gun towards me. The only thing I remember is to shoot low at this close distance, like shooting a gopher. Too close, shoot low.

El Conchos gun jerked in his hand and exploded. The barrel was at an odd angle from the frame. He was staring at it with a surprised look on his face. His hand was bloody and there were blood specks up his arm and right shoulder. He didn't seem to be feeling any pain, just the surprised look. Then the cursing started.

"I'll get you for that," he said, reaching his left arm around behind him.

People on the sidewalk yelled that he had another gun in his belt. I didn't know what to do. He was definitely reaching for something, so I rushed him. I hit him as hard as I could with my shoulder. He was a big, heavy stout man, but in his drunken state, he couldn't keep his feet under him, so he went down on his back.

He was still struggling to get his other gun with his left hand. When he did, I jumped on his wrist with my high heeled riding boot, pinning his arm to the ground. He was hitting at my leg with his broken gun. He got the left gun cocked and shot across the street into the boardwalk.

I started stomping on his hand and gun with my other boot, when a loud voice said, "Drop the guns."

Finally, the law showed up, a big sheriff star with his gun on me. I tried to explain that this guy was shooting at me and I was only trying to defend myself.

"Drop it," he said again to me, so I laid my 45 on the ground.

"If I take my boot off of this guy, he will be shooting," I said.

So the sheriff pointed his gun at El Concho and said, "Drop it."

El Concho laughed. The sheriff finally got him disarmed. After looking at all his wounds, he told two guys to take him to the doctor.

I spent the night in jail worrying about my horses. I was told they would be taken care of at the livery.

The next morning a big well-dressed man came in with a small badge on his shirt that read "Texas Ranger." The sheriff explained what he knew about the shooting.

The big man came over to the cell. He had a big mustache, wider than his face and a big white Stetson.

He asked, "Are you the shooter?"

"Yes," I said, "after being shot at by the shooter."

The ranger turned and asked the sheriff where the shooter was.

The sheriff told him, "Down at the doc's."

"Did you identify the shooter?" the Ranger asked.

"Nope, never seen him before," the sheriff said.

The ranger walked to the desk and pulled out a bunch of posters from one drawer. He found one and laid it in front of the sheriff and asked if this guy looked familiar.

I could see El Concho on it.

"Well yeah, could be," the sheriff replied.

"You have got the wanted man outside of jail, unguarded, and the assault victim in jail," the ranger retorted.

The sheriff, obviously stunned, didn't know what to say. He got up and came over to unlock the jail door but stopped.

He asked me, "You did shoot in self defense, didn't you?"

"Yeah," I said. "What did the witnesses say?"

"Well yeah, that's pretty much what they said."

"Did any of them have any other story?" I asked.

He finished unlocking the door and said, "Well, no."

"I was just going by what I saw, one man shoots, and the other standing over him with a smoking gun."

I looked at the ranger, who had a half smile grin on his face.

Looking at the poster, the sketched picture was bad, with little resemblance to the man. El Concho was heavier and had full facial hair.

"We've been after El Concho for years," the Ranger said. "He's an across the border bandit with twenty some in his gang. They mostly rustle cattle and horses across the border. That's why we can't catch him. This is pretty far north for them to venture. Apparently, his horse went lame and he threw one of the gang members off his horse and rode to Sonora."

"Yeah, and got drunk," I said.

"Right, the gang at this point had enough of El Concho. As soon as he started drinking, they all mounted up and left him horseless."

"Oh great," I said, "and there I was with my horses."

"The bounty is two hundred fifty dollars for information to arrest and convict," Ranger Smith said. "We'll need your full statement on what happened. Then after a conviction, you can get your bounty."

From jail to a bounty, what next, I thought.

"I just want to get out of here with my horses. I have to head north, so if there is any reward money, maybe you could give it to your school and church."

"Okay," Ranger Smith said, "sign a statement to that and you're free to go."

I grabbed my guns, shook his hand, and headed out the door.

Seven dollars to board my horses, but they were safe. Worth it, I guess.

Bob and Noa had come to town looking for me. They were waiting for me at the stable.

"Pack up," I said. "Let's get out of here."

We rode hard the rest of the that day and all night. We took to riding at night and sleeping during the day. In this country, that worked out good for avoiding the sun and trouble. This country was wild I thought. You have to fight for everything you own, just the opposite of back home in Dakota. Maybe a lack of law and order, I thought.

I had my prize stallions and now it was just a matter of getting them home. Noa had already gentled one of the mares to the point that he was riding it. We got the expensive horses I was after, but we were a long way from home.

I started to think about all the people that warned me about the outlaw trail and now I really knew what they were talking about. I wondered what could happen next.

CHAPTER 25

Riding at night and finding shade to rest during the day worked out well. In this dry country with little cloud cover the moonlight was bright enough that we had no trouble following the main trail.

I was relieved when we were out of Texas and well on our way back to Shilo Ranch. We avoided the larger settlements and towns which always drew attention to the horses. People around here knew good horse flesh and were always inquiring if they were for sale.

I had my bill of sale and had to show it a couple of times to law enforcement officers, I think mostly because of the Indians, but I could never have done this on my own. In fact, Bob and Noa were the only two people I knew that could have accomplished this with me. Noa worked training the new horses every day.

One day Noa pointed off to the southwest. I could see nothing.

"Indians trailing us," he said.

"How many?"

"Maybe ten, he held up ten fingers."

"They want the horses?" I asked.

"I think so, I don't know what else."

Riding at night and camping in the daylight threw them off. They couldn't sneak up on us. They followed at night waiting for us to stop.

We were getting closer to the mountains every day and the settlements became more numerous, so the Indians would have to make their move if they were going to, and they did.

As the sun came up, we had about twenty Indians behind us in a semicircle, the closest ones being about a quarter mile away. We were out in the open so there was no cover to run to and take a stand.

I didn't know how dangerous they were. Noa and I looked at each other. I could see the concern on his usually jovial face. Trouble, I guessed. How far would they go to get some of these horses?

Then Noa said, "Shoot them."

I didn't want to start anything if I didn't have to.

"Let them know they are too close," he said. "Your smokeless rifle will shoot that far. You could scare them by showing them how powerful it is, that it's "big medicine." I'm sure they haven't seen anything like that."

"Is that our only choice?" I asked Noa.

"I think they will creep closer until they see their chance," he said.

Sure enough, they kept inching closer. I became jumpy and sweat ran down my forehead. I noticed Noa was sweating also. We were only three men trying to protect a very valuable string of horses and it seemed like everybody wanted them. Finally, I told Noa and Bob to each take a string of horses and go on ahead and if you see a settlement, make a run for it. I'll drift back and see what happens.

My nerves were on edge and the sweat was running. They kept on coming. Finally, I decided I had to do something before they got within the range of their old guns. With my rifle fully loaded and reloads sticking out of every pocket, I turned and fired a shot that blew up dirt in front of the biggest bunch of them. The Indians were unimpressed, but some of their horses were obviously not veteran war ponies. Several of them jumped and turned and bucked. Scare the horses. I emptied the rifle, reloaded, and fired. I could tell my range now and was able to kick up dirt right under them.

I kicked Bart hard, something I usually never do because he needs no encouragement. We were stretched out. Bob and Noa were a long way ahead of me and running too. One Indian emerged from the dust on a good horse that was obviously fearless.

I told Bart, "Okay, let's see what you can do."

About then a rifle shot behind me. I turned to see a muzzle blast from his rifle which was pointed directly at me.

I lost my head, which I swore I would never do again. I turned and emptied the Winchester directly at him. Luckily for the both of us, trying to hit a running horse from a running horse is almost impossible, but then there's always luck. I obviously didn't hit. Suddenly, his horse veered off the trail and into some rocks and brush and down he went. It didn't look good.

By then I caught up to Bob and Noa. Noa pointed to smoke coming from over a low hill, a settlement most likely. We wasted no time getting there.

It was a small settlement of a few venturesome souls who came clear out here on the plains to find unclaimed land. They only had one business establishment and that was a combination general store, feed store, restaurant, and saloon. I went to get some much needed supplies.

I learned that this was what was considered the edge of Indian territory. I told them our story and that I was very aware of that. After supplying up we headed northwest towards Shilo Ranch. Luckily for us, the settlements became more frequent and the Indians less frequent.

My mind could relax somewhat now. I could think about what we had been through. I wondered if

I would have ventured on this trip if I had known what we were really in for. But I had my prize horses and none of us had any bullet holes in us. I couldn't help thinking we were more lucky than smart.

Should I do this again? Looking at the six Texas quarter horses, I couldn't help but think that these may have to be the entirety of the start of my pure-bred quarter horse herd.

I still held out hope of somehow getting some of the mountain mustangs. "Shoot the stallion," was the only way, everybody said. But shooting such a magnificent, beautiful animal rode hard against any horse loving cowboy.

We were enjoying the cooler weather after sweating through Texas, but now it was getting cold at night. The Indians had this figured out. They would drape a blanket over their shoulders and skirt it around the horse, so the horse's body warmth came up into the blanket and kept both horse and rider warm.

We headed to Shilo Ranch and the dream of adding a few mountain mustangs to my ranch stock.

CHAPTER 26

We ran into snow well before we got to Shilo Ranch. Noa had trained the four quarter mares by now so we were also riding them, which helped us make good time back to Shilo.

Slim was the only one there. Jesse was off helping a stagecoach that had gotten stuck in the snow. Slim still had some of the elk meat we had gotten on our previous visit. He knew how to make an excellent roast with lots of thick gravy. What a relief from all the beans we ate down south. I noticed how Bob and Noa had taken to white man's food. I think I could see a little weight gain on both of them.

For the next two days, we helped around the ranch and slept. We were definitely worn out from our ordeal. Slim laughed when he heard our whole story of Texas.

"I'm surprised you only ran into that much trouble," he said. "What did we tell you?"

"Yeah, I guess," I said, "but we got what we went for."

"Yeah," Slim agreed. "You have the beginnings of a hell of a herd. Horses of that quality are pretty rare around here."

"And in Dakota," I added.

After two days, Jesse returned, saying they had gotten the stage to a lower elevation and thinner snow where it could get through.

"Well, you got back just in time. The snow should have brought the mustangs further down the mountain," Jesse said.

Great, I thought. We are going after them. I knew we couldn't do it ourselves.

"Great," Slim said, "the stage won't be running for a while because of the snow, so I can go with."

"We'll need all the help we can get," I said, "but somebody's got to stay here to watch the horses. I didn't go through all of that and get my prize stock just to lose them."

"Matt, Slim's younger brother, and the cook will be here," Jesse replied.

"How old is Matt?" I asked.

"Twelve."

"He's watched the place before by himself," Slim said. "Besides, nobody'll come up here in this snow."

"Yeah," Jesse added, "we'll only be gone a day and a half, two at the most."

"Okay," I said. "It will definitely help to have all five of us up there."

Jesse brought up the subject of whether we wanted to try to shoot the stallion or not.

"Wow, is that our only choice?" I asked.

"Nobody's ever gotten any of them without causing confusion in the herd and cutting some of them out," Slim said.

After thinking about it, I said, "Jesse, we'll have to bring that big Sharps rifle."

"No," he said, "that's for a stationary target. I doubt that stallion will stand still long enough for that kind of a shot. He may have been shot at before, so the next best thing would be that .30 Winchester you have."

"Okay," I said, "if that's our only chance."

"We may each have to take two horses, too," Jesse said. "It's going to be tough getting up to that pass in this snow. That's the bad news. The good news is that the mustangs should be below there by now, so we'll have a better shot at them."

"Okay, when should we go?" I asked.

"If the snow breaks tonight, we'll leave in the morning," Slim said.

"So let's pack our gear and get the horses ready," Jesse suggested.

In the morning it was clear and cold.

"Perfect," Slim said, "the storm has blown clear away."

We ate and packed in silence, all eager for the chase.

Well prepared, we headed up. The further up we got, the colder it was. Bob, Noa and I took out our bed roll blankets and draped them around us and our horses.

Jesse and Slim scoffed at us and we, in return, laughed at them.

"I thought you northern boys could handle the cold," they said.

The going got tough, the snow was belly deep on the horses in places, and it didn't look like we would get to the top by nightfall.

Before long, Slim pulled out his blanket and draped it around him and his horse. I could tell his fingers weren't working by the way he fumbled with the blanket.

"Your fingers could freeze so hard, they could fall off," I said.

He said nothing. We went on. Then Jesse did the same thing.

"You boys hang around us northern boys long enough, you'll learn something," I said.

Slim cracked a smile and Jesse shook his head.

We got to the pass just before dark. Luckily, the wind was out of the west so we could build a fire and the smoke would drift away from the mustangs.

Noa snuck out to the valley to scout it out.

"No horses in sight," he said, "not even tracks. The valley was blown mostly clear of snow."

He thought some places were clear of snow and grass showing where horses could graze. Slim thought they were below us, driven down by the storm. There was nothing we could do till morning anyway, so we fed the horses and ourselves to get our energy up for the morning chase.

I was checking the Winchester when Jesse asked if it would work in this cold.

"Oh, it will work," I said. "I don't know if my fingers will work.

"We'll be lucky to get any," Jesse said.

"Oh, I know that. Good horses are hard to get."

"That's why they're still here," Slim said. "All the easy ones are caught. I don't have to tell you how valuable horses are out west. These are still here because they have outsmarted every man that's tried to catch them."

"Yeah, right," I said, "outsmarted by a horse."

Bart seemed to look at me and nicker.

None of us slept much that night. We all huddled around the fire with the horses. We ate all our food and drank all our coffee. We fed the grain to the horses. About five or six in the morning, Noa came back in and said they were there, just starting back up the mountain, strung up and down the valley.

"Wow," I said. "We need a plan. We'll only get one shot at this."

"You'll only get one shot at that stallion," Jesse said.

I was shaking. All of us were shaking. I don't know if it was from the cold or the excitement. Those horses represented thousands of dollars to us.

"We have to wait until we have some sunlight," Slim suggested.

"Yeah, and we need to take a running start from back here to surprise them," Jesse said.

Noa shook his head in approval.

It seemed like it took forever for the sun to come up. We saddled the horses. Bob said we could leave the others untied and they would follow us down the mountain. We could barely see.

I had a hard time holding Bart. He seemed to sense what was going on and wanted to go. He seemed aware of the horses in the valley even though he couldn't see them. I mounted up and got my gloves on because the steel on that rifle was cold.

I looked back. Everybody was mounted. Jesse and Slim pointed and mouthed "Go!"

I didn't even spur Bart, he took off on his hind legs. We were all moving. We broke out into the valley and there were two hundred fifty to three hundred fifty horses strung up and down the valley. Surprisingly, the snow muffled our hoof beats, so we were well into the valley before they knew it.

Then I saw him up the valley on a rise. He was about to rear up and sound a warning when I shot. I missed of course, but in the clear, cold, still air, the rifle blast was like an explosion and the bullet hit the rock wall on the other side of the canyon causing an equally loud blast. The explosive sound in the still of the morning was so unexpected that it caused confusion and the mustangs didn't know what to do.

Bart and I were speeding across the valley. I don't know what came over me, a feeling of euphoria or a high. It felt like I was on top of the world. I felt elation and excitement like I had never felt before. Was it that it looked like we were going to get some of the mountain mustangs? Maybe so.

They were yelling behind me. I still had a distance to go to cut off the lower mustangs.

"Shoot!"

Yeah, the noise. The mustangs could still slip by.

"Shoot!"

I shot again at the rock wall and again an explosive sound echoing and again the mustangs turned away from the scary sound. I kept shooting and they kept backing down. The rest of them started shooting too. Wow, we were herding horses with gunfire. We finally reached the other side of the valley.

Bart put his head down and blew hard. In my elation, had I pushed Bart too hard? I jumped off and loosened the cinch, so he could breathe.

Bob saw what was going on and retrieved our other horses. We were firing from the ground. The mustangs were in their element and would be gone if they got past us. I got my second horse from Bob and we frantically rode back and forth to keep the mustangs below us, shooting as fast as we could reload.

We finally had them stopped. One big dark stallion came out of the herd to challenge us. He realized the big speckled gray stallion had gone up with the rest of the herd and he was now the new leader. He pawed the ground, then reared up and nickered loudly.

I heard something behind me. It was Bart. He had answered the challenge. He seemed to have gotten his second wind. Bart was not as big, and I had run him hard. The cinch on his saddle was loose.

That damn stallion that I loathed so much may be going to save the day.

They came at each other, teeth first. All the other horses seemed to just stand and watch. That big mustang stallion looked tough. I felt I had to intervene. I kicked the mare that I was on, but she was very reluctant to get near the fray.

I had my lasso in one hand and the .45 in the other. Maybe this was the stallion I was going to have to shoot. They were yelling behind me. I couldn't tell what they were saying, but I had to help Bart even if it meant shooting a mustang stallion.

Bart got in the first bite, drawing blood. The mustang only ground his teeth on hard old saddle leather. He stopped in surprise. By then I got between them. He started to bite at the mare. My lasso struck hard across his nose at the same time as Slim's bullets grazed his chest, blood in both spots, but he seemed unfazed.

Bart went after him again. In all my years around horses, I had never seen two big stallions fight like this. They seemed to want to fight to the death. I didn't want to hit Bart, so I couldn't get a clear shot.

Jesse rode in and tried to ram the stallion with his horse, while he tried to rope him. The lasso only went around his nose. The big stallion fought to get the rope off. It was just enough time for Bart to put his teeth to the mustang's hind quarters, drawing blood in several spots. I rode by Jesse just as the mustang shook the rope off. I pulled the trigger at the same time as Jesse yelled, "No!"

Dead silence. Nothing happened. I was out of ammo. Time stopped as if everybody stopped to take a breath. But Bart broke that and came at the stallion full speed.

"Stop Bart!" Jesse yelled.

As he came by me, I jumped from my horse onto his back. I pulled his head to one side as hard as I could. He wanted to fight, so his teeth came for my leg. I lifted his head to his back and talked to him. I turned him away from the other stallion.

Jesse, Slim, Bob, and Noa surrounded the stallion and roped him. He fought mightily, but with four ropes on him he couldn't do much.

I kicked Bart into a run as I always did to tire him out. I rode at the mustangs to get them headed down the valley. He tired fast after all he had been through. I kept talking to him and told him he had won.

They rode the other stallion down to the mustangs and they seemed to sense he was beat. They still didn't want to go down the valley.

I said, "Turn him loose. If we chase him down, I bet they'll all follow."

I stopped and cinched up Bart. I needed to stay on him now because I didn't know what he would do if he saw that stallion again.

Slim said, "We need to cut them over to the next valley so we could head them down into the Shilo pasture and corrals."

Noa said, "I will take our extra horses on ahead and see if they will follow over the ridge. Sometimes, if horses see horses ahead of them, they will follow."

"Okay," Slim said. "Good idea."

Noa went on ahead and they seemed to follow. I heard Jesse yelling and whooping. I looked at him. He had a big grin and pointed at the mustangs. Then Bob did the same thing. Yeah, white man's sign language, thumbs up. We had done it if we could get them to the corrals at Shilo.

CHAPTER 27

They didn't herd very well. But being in a valley, they couldn't get away. So, with some prodding and more gunfire we finally got them over the ridge. We got them to the first barbed wire fence of Shilo pasture. I couldn't believe it. They jumped the fences like deer. Would the six foot high corral fences hold them? I could see them all jumping six feet and disappearing down the mountain. I rode over to Jesse who had seen the fence jumping too and asked if the corral fences were going to hold them.

"If they jumped those, they would be super horses."

Noa in the lead saw what happened. He and Matt kept them back from the corrals. I rode over to Noa.

Noa said, "If we feed them grain, they will stay."

So Noa and I cut out four of them and put them into a corral. He turned out to be right. They ate and didn't challenge the 6' high corral. Shilo Ranch had lots of corrals because they kept a lot of horses for the stage line.

After we took turns eating, Bob, Noa, and Matt offered to camp out and keep an eye on the new mustangs. We split them up and put them with other horses. After they ate and drank, they seemed to settle down. All except the dark stallion, who ran around and bit at the corral gates that held them in.

Slim brought out a bottle of whiskey, "I need something to calm my nerves," he said.

"My nerves are fine," Jesse said, looking at him sympathetically and grabbed the bottle saying, "but this calls for a celebration."

He took a drink and handed it to me. I wasn't much of a whiskey drinker, but for some strange reason, I felt compelled.

My nerves were ravaged and I was cold. I had to sip. I was not used to it.

Jesse slapped me on the back and said, "Come on, turn her up, let's celebrate. You know what we did today?"

"Yeah," I said. "We did something."

"Slim here has lived his whole life on this ranch and never before put a rope on one of those wild mustangs," Jesse quipped.

"You've been here damn near that long and have you ever before today put a rope on one?" Slim returned.

"Nope," Jesse replied, getting a little tipsy.

I was really beginning to feel good myself and took a couple of more sips.

I asked Slim and Jesse if they had the same euphoric feeling as I had when we were chasing the mustangs at the top.

"Yeah," Slim said. "It's the same feeling you have now. At high altitudes, the air is thinner. It's the same as having a shot of whiskey."

"Oh yeah," I said. "I didn't know that. I guess that explains it then."

"Yeah, you low land mule farmers wouldn't know that," Jesse replied.

"Yeah, I guess that would explain you living up here," I shot back.

He took a poke at me and I turned over his chair. We were both laughing when Matt came in to get something to eat.

"How's it going out there?" I asked.

"Great, except for that dark stallion. He's running around and causing trouble."

"We can fix that," Jesse said, pulling out his knife.

"Yeah, maybe," I said. "How many did we end up with?"

"Noa said sixty four."

"Okay. How many stallions?"

"Three," Matt replied.

"Three," we all said in unison, and then started laughing uncontrollably.

Matt went in to get something to eat.

If Jesse cuts one, that leaves two.

"Could that be right?" Jesse asked. "Out of sixty four horses, we only got three stallions?"

"I'd trust Noa would know. He knows horses better than anybody I've been around."

"So do we want to cut one?" Jesse asked.

"I don't know. What do you think, Slim?"

"He'll be a tough one to break," Slim said.

"Well, Bill here has that black devil, and he seems to ride him okay," Jesse added.

"Yeah," I said, "but that was a lot of work and besides, he was my only stallion for a while."

Matt finished eating and came out to watch the horses.

"Send Noa down, would you?" I asked him. "He'll know what to do. I bet he needs a drink too."

"Okay," Matt said as he walked away. "He's already trying to ride one of the mustangs," Matt called back.

"Wow, he's a horseman," Slim said. "Where did you find these Indians anyway?"

"Montana," I said. I told them the whole story about getting quarter horses from the Texans in Montana.

"They were just hanging around there, so I put them to work moving the horses home and they have been with me ever since."

"Wow, you trust them?" Jesse asked.

"We've been through hell together and they are still here, so yes," I said. "They're after what I'm after, the finest horses we can find."

"What are you going to do now?" Slim asked.

"We'll take my horses and try to get them back to Montana if I can."

"I'm going to Montana with you," Jesse suddenly said. "I've always wanted to go there, and this is the time. Besides, you'll need help wrangling those horses up there."

"Yeah," I said, "that'd be great, but as wild as these mustangs are, we'll probably need at least one more wrangler."

"I'll see if I can find somebody," Jesse replied. "I'm going to take ten of my cut out to western Montana and sell them to the miners. I hear they're paying top dollar."

"Good idea," I said. "I'll cull out what I don't want and go with you. I've never been to western Montana either."

"How long is that going to take you?" Slim asked. "We have a bunch of new horses to break you know."

Just then Noa came in. I handed him the bottle. He got a big smile on his face, mumbled something, and tipped up the bottle.

"Sixty four mustangs?" I asked.

He shook yes and held up six and four fingers.

"But only three stallions?" I asked.

He shook again and held up three fingers.

"How many you got broke?" I asked.

251

He laughed and held up one finger. We laughed.

Jesse said, "You got a long way to go."

"Too tough," he said, "too wild."

"Should we cut that dark stallion?" I asked.

"I think so," he said, "otherwise too much trouble."

"What Indian language is that anyway?" Jesse asked.

I laughed, "English."

"What? No!"

Without thinking about it I had been around Noa so long that I could understand him as well as Bob did.

They laughed. I shrugged.

Before the night was over, the dark stallion was gelded.

We stayed at Shilo for another week working hard to break the new horses. My half, thirty two mustangs, plus the six quarter horses were a good winter's work. We'd be herding near fifty animals to Dakota. We found another rider, Nick Miller, who wanted to see Montana too.

The first part of the trip was busy, trying to keep the mustangs together. They didn't herd well, so we were constantly chasing them back in.

We only had trouble with Indians twice. We bluffed them out the first time. They wanted some of our horses for crossing their land. The second time there were twelve of them. I ended up giving them a cow we picked up for camp meat. A cheap price to pay to get out of that, I thought.

I started riding one of the mustangs that we broke. It was an old mare but still had good stamina.

"Four riders behind us," Noa said one day.

I pulled back and sure enough, four armed men seemed to be following our trail. I rode back to the herd and told Noa to keep an eye on them and let me know if they get any closer.

They got closer, so I decided to take a side trail over Rocky Point. The trail was shorter, but a rough climb. If they followed us there, I would know they were after the horses.

Near the top of Rocky Point, I pulled off and hid in some rocks. Sure enough, here they come. I waited until they were within rifle range, but fired a revolver shot when I jumped out. The Winchester was dead center on the first big guy, obviously the leader. I totally surprised them. They didn't know what to do.

"What your boys doin' up here?" I asked. "Nothing up here."

Silence, and then one of them said, "We're heading north for work."

"What kind a work?" I asked.

He shrugged.

"Aint no work up north this time of year. Nobody hires in winter."

"Maybe we're going up to look for gold," the first big guy said.

"Maybe your stories aren't jiving too good," I said. "Maybe you're following these horses so you can rustle them."

"Wild horses are anybody's horses," he said.

"Oh yeah, wild horses with shod horses amongst them?"

"Ranches lose shod horses all the time," he returned.

The fourth one back had been easing back until he was halfway behind a rock. He grabbed his revolver and got off a quick shot. I peppered him with rock fragments and quickly turned the rifle on the other three who all had their hands up. They were too close for comfort.

"I think you boys better drop them all right there," I said. "Rifles and revolvers."

"You can't leave us out here without guns," one of them said.

"Oh, I'll give them back, just as soon as I know we'll be safe."

"Where you going to give them back at?" one asked.

"I'll leave them at the sheriff's office in Miles City," I said. "You can pick them up there."

The looks on their faces told me what I wanted to know. They weren't going to pick up their guns at no sheriff's office.

"You boys head right back down that trail. Find your buddy. He's still got a gun just in case you need to shoot a rattlesnake or something."

As they headed back down the trail, I grabbed their guns and headed back after the horses. I no more than got down on the flat before I heard eight quick shots. A rifle, I thought, quite a ways away.

The bullets landed all around me. The last one struck my back, right under my right shoulder blade. I fell off Bart and laid low on the ground, hoping the shooting had stopped. I looked up and saw nothing. The shooter was obviously in the rocks leading to Rocky Point. I had no cover I could get to, so I tried to whistle Bart back over between me and the shooter. Better him than me.

Loud hoof beats were coming. Who could that be? I had my .45 so I got it out. The bullet hadn't penetrated but it sure stung. I slowly turned and saw Noa and Nick ride up. They had been trailing the herd and heard the shots.

Noa pointed. I turned to see the shooter bolt out of the rocks and ride the other way. I was sure it was the fourth guy.

"Get my horse. I'm going after him," I said.

"No, you got blood on your back," Noa replied.

"It didn't penetrate," I said. "It's just a wound."

I could feel blood run down my back, and I cringed with pain getting off the ground.

"That doesn't look good," Nick said. "You don't want me to go after him?"

"We better get the horses headed north."

"Where'd you get all those guns?" he asked.

"I got all their guns except this one. He got away."

I ripped my red flannel sleeves off. Noa put one against the wound and tied the other around my chest to hold it.

Noa said, "Come on, boss, we better go get some whiskey to put on it."

I smiled. Was it that bad or was Noa just playing to find out where the whiskey was hidden? Noa was cleaning the wound when Jesse rode up.

"Go ahead, keep them moving. I'll tend to him," Jesse said. "How bad does it hurt? Have a drink of this. It'll help."

"It's okay," I said. "Noa found the bullet. It didn't penetrate, so I'm fine."

"I think we better get to Miles City and have the doc look at this," he said.

It stung pretty good now after the whiskey was on it, so I said, "Let's go."

CHAPTER 28

Everything was going well. So I rode on ahead to get my doctoring done in Miles City, supply up, and get back to heading those horses north. I didn't feel normal, like myself, so that bullet must have done more to me than I thought.

I got into town and asked the first person I came to about the doctor's office. He pointed down the street. On my way I noticed the sheriff's office. I decided to drop the guns there first. I entered to find a deputy seated at the only desk in the place. I dropped all the guns on the desk and pointed at the bullet hole in the back of my coat.

"Where'd you bury them?" he asked.

"Didn't shoot them," I said. Then I told him the whole story.

"So, you haven't seen the doctor yet?"

"No," I said

"You better go, then come back and swear out the complaint and we'll need a full description."

"Okay," I said and headed to the doctor's office.

The doctor said that luckily it hit a rib. Otherwise, it may have penetrated the chest and then I would have been in trouble.

"The rib's not broke, but it's most likely cracked. It'll be painful for a while. It'll heal up if it doesn't get infected."

He applied some red liquid that looked like blood, which stung worse than the whiskey.

"The more it stings, the more it's killing the germs," he said. "Keep it clean and put this on it every day."

He handed me the rest of the bottle and some sterile cloth. He wrapped it and sent me on my way. The deputy had the paperwork ready for me to fill out.

He said, "Those rustlers will never come for these guns, so you may as well take them. Looks like you earned them anyway," he said after looking at my back. "Besides, we have a room full of confis-cated guns we don't have anything to do with."

"Oh yeah? You have that much trouble around here?" I asked.

"We're the only law for miles around here," he said. "Before that, the gun was the law. So yes, it'll be a while before law and order comes to this country."

I couldn't help thinking about how different it was back in Dakota. People there wouldn't believe how wild it was just a few hundred miles west of them. I wondered what was to become of this wild, law-less country.

At the general store, I found out Pem was out of town, so I thought I would catch up with him on the return trip. Besides, I was antsy to get those horses home and safe. Bart had a big load with the supplies and guns I had confiscated.

The further north we got, the deeper the snow got. Nick complained he was from the south and had never had to deal with snow and cold like this. I told him to wait a couple of months and it would be beautiful.

Noa and Jesse applied the red disinfectant to my wound. After a couple days it felt better.

We could see in the snow that we weren't being followed. So unintentionally, we let our guard down. They hit us on the third night out of Miles City. We were all exhausted after driving through the deep snow. Everybody but Noa had fallen asleep. He was out riding guard duty. I was awakened by gun fire, lots of gun fire. The mustangs began to run. Jesse and I mounted and were after them. It was about an hour before we had them cornered in a small box canyon. Bob came over and asked where Noa was.

"I don't know. He's not around?"

"No," Bob said.

"You guys watch the horses. I'll go check on him," I said.

Noa was crawling out of a snowbank he dived into when the shooting started.

"You okay?" I asked.

He nodded yes. I pointed to his horse laying in the snow with several bullet holes.

Wow, they meant business. If Noa hadn't jumped off, they would have got him too.

Noa pointed to the northwest and said, "They stampeded the mustangs and grabbed the quarter horses and headed that way."

I looked with alarm into the trees where the quarter horses had been tethered. They were gone. My heart sank. I had to go after them. I had come too far and paid too much to let them go.

"How many?" I asked Noa.

He held up four fingers.

"Could it be those same four we had trouble with before?" I asked him.

"I think so, yes," he replied, shaking his head.

"Not your fault, Noa," I said.

I thought we had scared those guys off. Besides, I was the one who let my guard down getting this close to home. I rode back to the herd and yelled at Bob to take Noa a horse. I found Jesse and told him what happened.

"I'm going after them," I said and asked him to get the herd to Williston. "Noa and Bob know the way, but I should be able to catch up to you by then."

"Yeah, if those outlaws don't shoot you full of holes," Jesse replied.

"I plan on being really careful and if it looks too dangerous, I'll get a sheriff and a posse to go after them."

"Okay," he said skeptically. "Be careful."

I loaded up and rode hard. They were easy to follow in the snow, four shod horses and my unshod quarter horses.

I needed to cool down and think this out. Four against one, four very dangerous men. That's probably why they thought they could get by with this. No one man would come after them, but they didn't know what I went through to get those quarter horse stallions. My only hope was to surprise them. I had my .30 Winchester and two Colt .45s, more than enough fire power to take out two or three of them before they knew what hit them.

Wow, was I actually thinking about shooting men, maybe from an ambush and maybe killing them? I never thought it would come to this.

Thinking back on it a lot of people told me that this was outlaw country, and that possession was ten-tenths of the law. Yeah, because there was no law out here. You were left to protect your own possessions. I had lots of time to think as I followed their trail.

They were headed northwest and as near as I could tell would reach the big river at some point. As far as I had ever heard, there was nothing out here, no settlers or settlements had come to this part of the country. Probably the big cattle herds came here to graze in the summer, but this was winter and there was nothing around. Yeah, good outlaw country, no law around.

A man could get killed out here and rot away and nobody would be the wiser. I thought back on the stories of bodies that some would come across on the prairie nobody could explain or identify. Maybe he was throwed from his horse and broke a leg and couldn't get anywhere for help. Yeah, and here I was on my outlaw horse who had tried to kill me more than once. He was dutifully following the tracks.

We went all night that night, I half asleep, wondering if Bart knew where he was going. But as the sun came up, he was dead on the trail. Was it horse following horses instinct, or could he smell them? Whatever, I thought, I would have to take back everything I said about old Black Bart. I guess I'd hold that until after we had recovered the quarter horses.

As darkness fell the second night, we topped a knoll. I could see something ahead. I was so tired I rode back down the knoll to some trees and started a fire to camp. Bart wanted his oats, maybe that was why he was performing so good. He knew I controlled the oats. The oats kept Bart strong and energetic.

I figured at this pace we should catch them tomorrow sometime, but what then? I needed to be cautious, surprise was my only advantage. I couldn't let them see me. They camped long every night. I was traveling faster than them so they couldn't be too far ahead.

I found their camp about five or six miles ahead, but before I caught them, the country got rough and then there was the big river. Their tracks led down to the river and across big sand bars. I could tell they knew their way around. This was a good crossing point, so they had been here before.

Wow, I thought, I was in their country, they knew the lay of the land. I could see their tracks cross the river and up a draw in the badlands on the north side of the river.

I waited and watched. The trail went up and disappeared in the hills beyond. If they looked back, they could see the river from their high vantage sight and also have a good shot at whoever was following them. I waited, wondering what to do. The sun came out and it was a clear day.

Should I risk it, go down there and become a perfect target in the middle of the river? I finally decided to go down river a ways and cross, so I wouldn't be so obvious to anyone in that draw. I was going to lose some time, but it was better than being discovered or shot.

When I got across, I went back upriver on the other side to resume the chase up the ravine. Bart was performing well, so I gave him more oats. Then

I thought I might get into a chase, me after them or them after me, so I fed Bart all the oats I had left. He shook his head up and down in approval.

"Yeah boy, well you may need all those oats."

He cocked his head to say let's go.

I could see nothing ahead as we headed up the ravine. I thought we would get out of the badlands and continue north. I could see the trail, but the out-laws turned left and followed a ridge parallel to the river headed west. The trail was not so apparent now, but these guys must know where they were going. I wished I did or if there were any towns nearby or even where I was.

This was certainly strange country to me, and in the middle of winter, too. What was I doing here? I was mad. I had legitimately obtained these horses and some outlaws had stolen them. And they shoot horse thieves, right? Wow, would it come to that? It had many times before from what I heard and read. The good guy doesn't always win, but he does in the penny dreadfuls.

The trees got thicker as we paralleled the river on the not too certain trail. Then we were in the trees and I could make out the thin trail. About that time, I smelled smoke. Their camp, I thought. That's funny, why would they start camp at midday?

I could tell by the smoke that I was close, so I led Bart off the trail and up into the trees and tied him. I made sure the .45s were loaded and that I had my pockets full of .30 caliber rounds.

As I made my way through the trees, the smoke got thicker and then the smell of side pork. Wow, did that smell good.

I finally got to a point that I could see. It wasn't a camp but a cabin, half logs and half clap boards, two small windows and a door. Smoke poured from the stovepipe chimney.

I couldn't see any horses, so I got within .30 Winchester rifle range and found a big tree. What do I do now? Just start shooting or what? I can't just start shooting people. I was sure these were the horse thieves, but what should I do? I had a good clear path back to Bart and out of here, but what then? How far was the nearest town and a sheriff and posse? Would they still be here?

They obviously knew of this cabin. Thinking about it, this was a perfect hideout. There was nothing else here, no gold miners, no ranchers, a perfect spot to hide.

Wow, I was looking at a real outlaw hideout. But now what do I do? The good guy in the penny dreadful went in firing and under the withering attack, the outlaws would surrender. Hah. I better be careful if these were those four men we encountered before. They looked mean and handy with their guns. But I was still mad. They stole my horses, my prize horses. I had to fight for them, but I had to give them a chance. I had to warn them before I opened fire. Yeah, if they shot back they were guilty right, then shoot.

I decided to yell at them and see what happened. I could hear them talking and banging pans around.

I yelled, "In the cabin, you stole my horses. I came to get them back. Send them this way and there'll be no trouble."

Silence.

So I lied, "I have the law with me. You don't have a chance."

To emphasize my point, I put a round through the roof. Before I knew it, all hell broke loose. The gunfire was deafening. The bullets hit the trees all around me. Splinters of wood hit everything around me.

This was it, I thought. I was mad. I got up and put all eight rounds into the cabin. I caught a glimpse of one of them running with a rifle from the back of the cabin up into the trees. He had pants and a red flannel shirt. He was obviously going to try and sneak up behind me. He didn't know I saw him. The trees were thick so he could get close before I would see him.

A shot or two came from the cabin, probably to draw my attention. I had to think fast, so I climbed up a tree so I would be above him. I could still see the cabin in case anyone else tried to sneak out. Then I saw him, jumping from tree to tree hoping to surprise me, but he was looking low. I was up the tree, out of sight. He looked confused but kept coming. He looked mean, like he would shoot somebody for no reason.

I didn't want to just shoot him, but I might have to. He came close and still didn't look up. He was right under me when I thought to shoot his rifle. Shoot low like at the gophers. His rifle jumped out of his hands as the bullet struck it.

The gunfire from the cabin was deafening again. I looked down and saw the outlaw actually fish his rifle out of the snow before he ran back. He had to know he was dead sights for me. Were these guys brave or stupid? Either way, they were dangerous.

I returned fire, emptying the Winchester into the cabin. A loud yell came from the cabin. The .30 smokeless obviously was going through the clapboards and somebody got hit. The gunfire continued.

I reloaded and got one shot off, as somebody tried to sneak back to what looked like a part of a corral. I didn't hit him but came close enough, he turned around. I finished unloading into the cabin and started reloading.

I pulled up to fire again, when a horse and rider headed straight away behind the cabin. The trail obviously continued west along the river. I put two well placed shots into the window. No return fire. Then two more horses and riders headed west.

The fourth guy made a run for the corral, but I was loaded, and my aim was getting better. He decided to turn back and no more than got behind the cabin before he was headed west on the trail. Four gone. Were there anymore? Only one way to find out.

I snuck through the trees to the edge of the cabin. I saw no activity, so I ran to the corner and snuck under the window to the door.

I yelled, "Come out or you're dead."

I remember reading that in the penny dreadful. It sounded good but got no results. I stuck my hat on my gun barrel and held it up to the window, something else I read in the penny dreadful. Nothing. No shot. I looked in to see nobody, just a whole pan full of cooking side pork.

How perfect, I thought. I was starved. I started eating. I saw the coffee pot on the floor with a hole in it. That was one shot I would regret. After eating a bit, I started shaking, suddenly realizing what had just happened. The place started getting spooky, a real outlaw hideout.

Then I saw it, blood on a chair and the floor. Suddenly, I wanted to get out of there, but I was tired. I threw the last piece of meat in my mouth and went outside. My quarter horses were in the corral with an old sway back mare, two saddles, and the Hackamore leads. The horses were all looking at me like where in the hell have you been? What's going on?

"We're getting out of here," I said.

They all came to the gate to get their leads put on, even the mare. I fed them the little hay that was there, saddled two of them and headed out, keeping a wary eye on the back trail. Somebody was hurt and probably mad at me.

I should have been elated that I had gotten my horses back, but I was tired and spooked and wanted to be out of there. I rode back to Bart. He was pulling at his bridle and was wild eyed. He had obviously heard all the shooting and also wanted to be out of there.

We went back to the main trail headed north. The trail was there but nobody had tracked through the snow in a long while. I hoped the trail led to some kind of town or settlement. I knew of nowhere else to go, so on blind faith we went north.

It was another all nighter, but Bart and the rest of the horses were too spooked to stop. I dozed in the saddle.

The next day, due to Bart, we were on the trail. It was a low overcast day and light snow was falling. I couldn't see very far, but we were in flat country.

I thought it best to stick to the trail because I had no idea where we were. I stopped once in a place the horses could see a little old grass. I let them eat while I made coffee. I didn't have anything else for them or me to eat so I was hoping to get somewhere. We were on an obvious trail, but whether it led anywhere, I didn't know.

Late in the day finally I came to some low hills and soon after that I smelled smoke. It had to be at least a ranch or something. Food, I thought. I'll pay anything. Buildings appeared out of the murk, smoke, and dim light. No people. I got that spooky feeling again. Were there people here or ghosts? No signs on any building, no saloon, no restaurant, nothing. Finally, I saw a barn like structure and figured it had to be the stable.

I pulled up and pulled the door open and said, "Hello?"

Silence.

"Anybody here?"

"What you want?" a voice came from inside.

No light. I couldn't see him.

"I'd like to put up my horses," I said, "grain and feed."

"Okay," he said. "You got two dollars?"

"Yes," I said. "Where am I?"

"You don't know?" he returned.

"No," I said. "I don't see any signs."

"Landusky."

"Landusky?" I repeated.

"Yeah," he said. "Nobody ever comes here, so everybody from here knows where they're at, and knows what buildings are what."

"What's here?" I asked.

"Used to be mining big time, now it's gone, so just the local ranchers and such. What are you doing here?" he asked, admiring my horses. "And where did you get these?"

"Texas," I said, "and I'm just passing through. Where can I eat and where is the sheriff's office?"

"That bright light building is the saloon. The sheriff, if you can call him that, will be playing cards at the back table. Can't miss 'im. They'll be the only ones in there. You can eat in the building just this side of the saloon. Beat on the door hard. They may be in the back."

"Okay, thanks," I said, handing him the two dollars.

He smiled and looked at the two dollars like he wasn't really expecting to get it.

CHAPTER 29

He was right. Other than the bartender behind the bar, there were five men playing cards at the back table. I walked up to them and asked who the sheriff was.

The man across the table said, "That'd be me," holding one side of his vest open revealing a silver star with Sheriff inscribed on it. "What you need?" he asked without looking up.

I told him about the horse theft, the chase, and shootout at the cabin. I explained how I thought the cabin was obviously an outlaw hideout because of its location.

"What kind of horses you got?"

"Oh, just some breeding stock I was taking home when they hit us."

"Where'd you get them?"

"Down," I almost said Texas but said, "south. I got a bill of sale for them," holding up the piece of paper.

Again, he didn't look up. He just went on concentrating on his card game. I didn't like the fact that he was more interested in my horses than the horse thieves.

"Well, you said you got your horses back."

"Right," I said, "but not without a fight."

"Where you headed for?" he asked.

"Back over to Dakota where I'm from."

By now I could tell the other four cowboys at the table were paying close attention to the conversation. I was beginning to feel not so comfortable. All these questions had nothing to do with the description or location of the horse thieves.

"We could get a warrant, might take about a week. Then we'd have to get a posse together."

"I don't have that much time," I said. "I have to be going."

"Okay," he said. "I'll take note of what you said and be on the lookout."

"Okay, thanks," I said, not knowing what to think of the sheriff's inaction.

I guess his card game was more important than horse thieves. Neither the sheriff nor any of them ever looked up, not even once.

I backed out of there, not knowing what to think. But hunger intervened and I headed to the eating place. A woman finally came to the door after I knocked hard.

She led me to a table and said, "Stew is all we got, it's heating."

After a while, she brought a big bowl of steaming stew with beef, potatoes, and carrots in a heavy broth. I was so hungry I thought it was the best food I'd ever eaten. She also had fresh bread with butter and milk. She looked tired and didn't talk much, like most people in this town.

I asked her what the next biggest town was east of here.

"Glasgow," she said.

"This road lead to it?"

"Follow it north till you hit the main east west trail. Head east and you can't miss it."

She walked away, uninterested in conversation.

I had heard of Glasgow and knew it was a good one hundred to one hundred fifty miles from home.

"Two bits," she said.

I laid down four bits.

"Must be rich," she said.

"No, just passing through," I said. "But could you put a big piece of that beef between two slices of that bread?" I asked.

She nodded and walked back to the kitchen and brought out the sandwich wrapped in wax paper. I tipped my hat and she said nothing.

I left having mixed emotions. Funny how people keep to themselves around here. That and the inaction of the sheriff made me a little spooked again, so

I decided to sleep in the barn with the horses. The stable boy was sleeping in a side room, so I went up to the hay loft and rolled out my bed roll on some hay.

I was so tired I couldn't even think about the situation anymore before I fell asleep. I figured I'd slept about five or six hours before the cold woke me up. The stable boy and horses were sleeping soundly.

I went down and got the fire going in the little stove, put coffee on. The commotion woke the horses who were all awake and restless about something. I gave them all another hand full of oats, as the coffee got hot.

I didn't know what time it was, but there were no lights in any of the buildings on the main street. The coffee and stove warmed me. As I thought about how strange this place was, I suddenly became restless to get out of there. The horses were all looking at me, so I saddled and bridled them all up and led them out the back door hoping nobody would see us leave. I left four bits for the stable boy, thankful that he hadn't awakened.

We moved through the corrals and up a back street to the trail headed north. After we were out of town a ways and it didn't look like we had awakened anybody, I put the horses into a fast pace to try to warm them up. It was cold, but the snow had stopped falling.

There was a silent fog that kept me from seeing very far. A dim glow was high overhead, a full moon, I thought. Then to add to the spookiness, a howling far off, not exactly like the coyotes I was used to. Maybe it was the wolves I'd heard about. I'd never seen one, but they were supposed to be bigger than coyotes. The horses were wild eyed and had their ears pricked every time the howling started. They were as spooked as I was.

I said, "Don't worry boys, I got the .30 Winchester out."

They all gathered in close to me. I didn't need the lead rope, these horses were staying with the herd, even the sway back mare that looked a lot better now. I think she just needed some good feed. Her back even looked straighter.

I changed horses often to keep them fresh. We were making miles. Eventually the sun came up to a cloudy, foggy day. I couldn't see far but the trail was obvious. About midday we hit the east west trail and headed east. I was amazed that I never came across any travelers or settlements. Everybody else except me was smart enough not to be out here in outlaw country in the middle of winter.

Then I thought if I did meet anybody on the trail, what was the chances of them being horse thieves? I pulled out the rifle and laid it across my saddle. Now I wasn't so sure I wanted to meet anybody, for I knew I was in outlaw country, with no people and no food.

I was sure glad I had that extra sandwich. It was cold, but good. I fed the rest of the oats to the horses, thinking it couldn't be that much farther to Glasgow. The horses stayed close to me, especially the quarter horses. They were in strange country and I had the oats and the rifle for the wolves.

It was very cold. We became comrades in survival, eight horses and one man. The eerie, spooky fog persisted all day. Not much sunlight to heighten the spirits. But we trudged on through the fog hoping at some point to come across human habitation, good or bad.

Night fell again, darkness. It began to seem like we were in a lost world with only me and the horses in it. Lucky for us the trail was very visible and easy to follow. Was it going to be another all nighter?

I seriously thought about stopping to make a camp, but the only place to sleep was in the snow. I was comfortable with my blanket draped around the horse and the warmth coming up into it. Without realizing it, I was so tired that I drifted off. I was getting accustomed to sleeping in the saddle.

It was time to switch horses, but there was frost on the other saddle, so I had to resaddle to another one. I drifted off for hours it seemed this time.

I woke up because I was sleeping so sound that I had lost the grip on the blanket and the cold hit me. We were stopped. All the horses huddled together. Then I heard it, the howling of the wolves or whatever they were was a lot closer. They were looking at me as if to ask what should we do now? Not thinking about it I spurred them on

I didn't know how long I'd slept or how long we had been standing and not moving. It was time to pick up the pace and get somewhere. Running the horses both warmed them and took their minds off our dire situation. We ran for a ways and then slowed to a trot. I didn't know what time it was. Someday I needed to get myself one of those time pieces, a pocket watch. I was usually pretty good at guessing the time, but with everything that had happened and the dark, foggy day that wasn't really day, I was lost as to what time it was.

I was thinking about that strange sheriff back there in Landusky, but I figured I didn't need to worry about him on my backside in this country; only survival and getting somewhere mattered. Next thing I knew I was awakening from another sleep, but we were still moving. Those wolves sounded hungry. Wow, I thought, so was I. The only animal instinct going on out here now was hunger.

I was so hungry I looked at my rifle and wondered what wolf meat would taste like. Then my thoughts turned to that sway back mare. I wondered with my love and admiration of horses, could I actually eat one? I heard the Indians had often done it. I was so hungry I couldn't keep my mind off the terrible thought.

We were in a valley, high hills on the left and trees on the right, most likely associated with the river. Just when I was wondering what kind of animals might be in those trees, I smelled it, a slight scent of smoke, I thought. But I sniffed hard and couldn't smell anything. Was my mind playing tricks on me? At this point anything could be possible. I noticed the horses were all looking forward with their ears perked. What were they sensing?

It was time to pick up the pace anyway, so I moved them out. After about a mile it happened; we rode right into a town. It was still dark, but there was light in several of the buildings and smoke coming from the stove pipes. Glasgow Hotel, a town with signs. I was back in the real world.

My whole body relaxed. I was beginning to wonder about my future, but we made it. The horses led us to the livery stable. Unlike the mustangs these quarter horses were domesticated and knew where they belonged. I stiffly got down, walked up, and opened the door to the stable making sure I wasn't dreaming. I walked in. The stable boy was still asleep but woke with all the commotion.

I asked him what time it was. He said coming along towards morning, he thought. I gave him two dollars and asked if he could oats and hay my horses.

"Sure can," he said, as we opened the big door to let them in.

"Glasgow Hotel, best place in town?" I asked.

"I've heard it is," he said, "but I've never stayed there."

I headed over to the hotel.

"We don't usually check in until 12:00 noon," the clerk said.

I threw two dollars on the counter.

He said, "But I think we can accommodate you sir."

I saw a door leading to the saloon on one side and the barber shop on the other. Under the barber sign read: "Bath 10 cents".

I grabbed my stuff and headed up the stairs. I didn't realize how stiff and sore I was until I climbed those stairs. Thinking back, I had been in the saddle for most of two and a half weeks, day and night, and all day before that.

The bed looked good. I laid down, but I was too pent up and stiff to sleep. The bath and maybe a shave. Two bits, hair and beard gone.

There was an oriental woman at the bath.

"Too early," she said.

I flipped her two bits.

"Water boil in ten minutes," she said.

I needed something to relax me. The saloon door was open. The barkeep was sweeping up.

"Too early for a drink?" I asked.

"Never too early or too late for a drink," he said.

I was the only one there and this was the first time in my life that I had deliberately walked into a saloon to get a drink. All the other times were when somebody else was passing a bottle. My family didn't drink, but I didn't know if any of them had ever been through what I had just experienced.

The oriental lady stuck her head in and said, "bath hot."

I threw down the whiskey and headed over.

"Whew, you need laundry too," she said.

I knew that.

"10 cents, leave outside your door."

"Okay," I said, almost falling asleep from the relaxing effects of the whiskey and hot bath.

I barely made it up to the room before passing out.

CHAPTER 30

I awoke confused. It was still dark out, no clothes. I remembered to lock the door. I opened it to find my clothes hanging neatly folded and pressed just outside the door.

I walked down to the clerk and asked what time it was. He pointed at the wall clock which said ten to six o'clock.

"In the morning or night?" I asked.

He laughed and said, "Night, not much daylight this time of year. You slept all through it."

Wow, hunger was my next thought.

"Food?" I asked.

"Next building, other side of the saloon," he pointed.

I headed over there, thinking this was the wildest ride of my life, but I was determined to get those horses home. Thinking about that, I stuck my head in the livery barn. They were so tired they were laying down.

"You don't have to worry about them mister, they're safe here," the livery boy said.

"Oh, I know that," I said. "I can see the barn well from my hotel room and my irons are loaded."

Thumbs up. Headed to eat.

"Something with beef, gravy, and potatoes," I said.

"Where's the sheriff's office?"

"Just down the street," she said, "but he should be here anytime now."

"Okay, thanks."

I was near done eating when he walked in.

"Sheriff," I yelled at him, "can I have a word with you?"

"Sure," he said in a friendly way, coming over and sitting down.

We shook and introduced ourselves.

"You're the one who came in with the string of horses from the west this morning."

"Yeah, news travels fast," I said.

"Nothing happens around here without me knowing about it," he said proudly. "Where'd you come from? Anybody west of here this time of year's got to have a good story."

So, I told him everything, the horse theft, the shootout, and the strange encounter with the sheriff in Landusky.

I was digging my bill of sale out and he held up his hand and said, "I believe you. This kind of stuff happens around here. First, let me tell you, anything west of here is outlaw country. You're lucky you got out of there with your hide. As for that sheriff in Landusky, he's riding a very thin line between the law and the outlaws. You're lucky you got out of there."

"Yeah," I said. "I left in the middle of the night and kept an eye on my back trail."

"That must have been a hell of a ride this time of year."

"Yeah," I said, "like nothing I've done before and never want to do again."

"Between here and this side of Havre is no man's land, mostly self-appointed sheriffs and rustlers. The wild bunch still operates out there. That might be who you encountered out at that cabin. One of the worst ones, Kid Curry, has been known to be around those parts."

"Bad?" I asked.

"He may have been in on the shooting of as many as ten lawmen and others."

He asked about the shootout. I told him the whole story

"You were safe in those trees and they were sitting ducks in that clapboard shack with your .30 Winchester going right through like that. Those guys have been in this business for a while. They knew when the odds were against them. Lucky for you, I'd say. I think I'd just rode out of there myself."

Then I told him the whole story of where the horses came from and what I had to do to get them.

"Well, I'd stay out of that country if I was you or next time bring enough guns to protect your property. As you know, the law is spread thin around here," Sheriff Lang added.

The next day was a sunny morning. I rode hard east, anxious to get back to the herd and see how they were coming. I realized I'd be riding right past Bob and Noa's family village on the river. I stopped and they remembered me as well and offered to let me stay the night, so I did. The smoked fish was as good as ever.

I helped them pull the fish net out of the ice hole. This was the toughest part of the process. The big catches were hard to pull out of the hole, especially on the ice. A horse with shoes was best for the job, so we used the mare I had gotten from the cabin. She had three shoes and nails in the fourth. She did well at pulling. Then the thought came to me. Why not? I hadn't paid anything for her, and she probably wasn't worth much, so I gave the horse to Bob's dad. The whole place was happy, more fish, more eating. I felt good about it. I believed I had gained friends for life.

They filled my big saddle bags with smoked fish before I left the next morning. I was really anxious to get back now. I lost a half a day there, so I set a high pace and we went on until well after dark to get to Williston that night.

No horses had arrived there. Being too dark to do any searching, I stayed the night. Early the next morning I was crossing the thinning ice of the big river. South of the river I ran into two riders coming north. They pointed me in the direction of a camped horse herd. There they were looking mostly intact, but not moving. The first thing I got hit with was Miller.

"Where the hell you been? I quit. I want my money."

I looked at Jesse and he just shrugged.

"Okay," I said.

"Eighteen days by a dollar and a half is twenty seven dollars you owe me."

Jesse was shaking his head yes. I dug out a twenty and a ten to give him.

"I aint got change," he said.

I gave it to him anyway and said the big bonus is getting them all the way to my place.

He calmed down and said, "I've had enough of this cold country."

He jumped on his horse, most likely headed to the nearest saloon.

"Other than that, it went pretty good," Jesse said. "What the hell took you so long?"

"Just a shootout with the wild bunch to get my horses back," I said.

"Ha," Jesse returned, "if that were true, you wouldn't be here."

By then Noa and Bob showed up. I told them the whole story. Noa and Bob were all ears, but I could tell Jesse was skeptical.

"Well, you say four guys stole those horses. Who do you think they were?" I asked.

"Oh, probably some low rate horse rustlers all right," he agreed, 'but the wild bunch?"

"Yeah, I don't know who they were, but the sheriff in Glasgow said Kid Curry from the wild bunch hung out in that area."

"Yeah, well I heard those guys hit what they shoot at," Jesse returned, "and I don't see any bullet holes in you."

"Only the one in my back that I can still feel," I said.

Noa said, "We only lost one mare and one colt, boss."

"One colt?" I said.

I turned and sure enough, in the herd were four foals. I had been disappointed that we had only gotten 32 mustangs, but I forgot about the foals. The mares were carrying foals.

My heart leapt, "We got more than thirty two mustangs."

"31," Jesse reminded me. "The one we lost was yours."

"Okay."

I went over to examine the new little horses and there he was. The only stallion among them was gray with spots on his hind quarters. Wow, I had a blood line from the big stallion and maybe a lot more I thought, looking over the herd.

"They fell through the ice and we got them all out except those two," Bob said. "That's why we stopped here. We wanted you here before crossing the big river."

We were close now, but we had to cross the "big" river.

"No lead ropes for the quarter horses?" Jesse asked.

"They're never going to leave me again," I said, "after what we've been through."

"Yeah, I can tell," he said. "They follow you around like a dog."

"We're going to have to string them out over the ice," I said, "to keep the weight spaced out."

We were able to do it without losing any. We spent the night in Williston to rest up. There were only four of us now, but the mustangs were herding better. Luckily for us, being away from their home range, they stayed together.

We left Williston in the morning, riding the mustangs that we had been able to break on the trail. Breaking wild mustangs was tougher than any other horses I had been around, but we worked them all the way home.

CHAPTER 31

We herded them into the farm late that day. Barney was there and opened the big corral gate. Noa saw what was happening and raced to the stack and started pitching green hay into the corral. I got the quarter horses in and they started eating. The mustangs noticed that and soon followed.

We had them. After everything that happened, they were in our home corral, a sight I was beginning to wonder if I was ever going to see.

By then Dad and Carl came running from the house. My dad and my two brothers stood against the corral fence and looked in wonder at all the new horses. I introduced Jesse all around and then announced that we were hungry as horses and could tell them everything over a hot meal. My family listened almost unbelievingly at our story bringing us up to getting all these horses here.

Carl asked, "What are you going to do now? Are you going to sell some? All those horses are pretty crowded in our small corrals."

Dad said, "We'll build more."

Then Jesse interrupted and said he and I planned to head west to the gold mines with several of them to sell.

"That should thin the herd enough so you can manage."

"Well," Dad said, "you only have two or three weeks til we start planting."

I said, "Bob and Noa are to stay here and train and break the mustangs while we're gone. And we should be back by then."

Carl asked, "You're going back out through that outlaw trail country again with even more horses this time?"

I looked at Jesse as if to ask are you sure we should do that?

We told them about the adventure except for the El Concho shooting and downplayed the shootout.

So Jesse almost spilled the beans by saying, "Well Bill here is becoming one of the best shots in the west and with me along, those outlaws better be the ones to watch out. Ha ha!"

I didn't want my family to know how dangerous things had gotten those couple of times that shots were fired. I didn't want them to worry about me, so I kicked Jesse in the leg under the table, and without missing a beat he said, "Besides, every little town out there has a sheriff now and law and order is coming quickly to the outlaw country."

Noa, Bob, and I smiled at him as if to say good catch.

Dad said, "Bill, let's go get a better look at those horses while everybody is eating apple pie."

I looked at him surprised, but he nodded at the door and said, "We have to figure out which ones we're going to cull out and send with you and Jesse out west for sale."

"Yeah, you're right," I said getting up.

The rest of them were having a good time talking and eating pie. As we left the house Dad had a letter with him.

"What's that?" I asked.

He showed it to me. It was from the Ranger in Sonora, Texas, addressed to me.

"I opened it," he said, "thinking you might be in trouble of some kind."

"What does it say?" I asked.

He handed it to me and said that El Concho, who I got into a fight with, had died of the gunshot wounds and that I didn't need to go back down there. They needed me to write back with my side of the story for the inquest. The reward money had been given to their school and church as I had asked.

"Wow, did Mom see this?" I asked.

"No, just me," he said.

He looked at me as if to ask what really happened down there. I never could keep anything from my dad. It was as if he could read my mind. I guess he was smarter than I was and knew there was more to the story. I pointed at the hind leg and the scar of the quarter mare.

"Where were you?"

"Standing right beside him," I said. Then I told him the whole story and how I had shot his gun in his hand and that the bullet fragments ricocheted and hit him in the arm and shoulder.

"He must have gotten an infection from the wounds."

"Well, he sounds like a real bad outlaw," Dad said trying to console me.

"Yeah," I said, "He was wanted for murder among other things."

"Well, the bad thoughts will go away with time," he said.

"But now you've got me worried about you. Maybe the penny dreadfuls aren't so fictitious after all," he laughed.

"It was the horses," I said. "Without them we'd have had no trouble."

"Horses are the lifeblood of the west," Dad said. "So they're always going to be valuable out there."

"Yeah, especially these," I said.

Just then Jesse, Bob, Noa, Carl, and Barney showed up and asked which ones we picked out to take out west. Dad and I looked at each other and shrugged.

"What have you two been so busy talking about that you couldn't get the job done?" Jesse asked.

Dad and I looked at each other and smiled. "Nothing."

The next day we culled the herd. I picked thirteen partially trained ones from my herd and Jesse had his ten. We would continue training and breaking them on the way out west.

I picked out ten others that looked older for sale to the Canadians.

"That should thin them down enough so we can feed them."

That night my mother gathered and washed my clothes. She asked what the hole was in the back of my shirt. "It looked like it had blood around it."

Thinking fast, I lied, "One of those wild horses backed me into a branch."

"Backed you into a branch," she replied skeptically.

I shrugged and asked, "What else could it be, Mom?"

CHAPTER 32

We headed out the next day. Mom and Dad were worried as we waved with Jesse's ten and my thirteen half-broke mountain mustangs. I gave Jesse all the details about everything that happened after the shootout by Landusky.

"The weather's getting better every day now, so we should be able to see what's coming," Jesse said.

We continued to work and train the horses as we went. I was plenty antsy about going through outlaw country again with valuable horses, but I knew I wouldn't miss a chance to see the western Montana mountains where all the gold was supposedly being dug up and, of course, see how well these horses sold out there. We first stopped at Glasgow and stayed at the Glasgow Hotel with the good food.

"Worth the money," I told Jesse.

He agreed. We walked in to eat at the restaurant by the saloon and there sat the sheriff. He remembered me.

"Say, I got a story to tell you about after you were here last time," he said as we sat next to him.

"A report came in that four men came into Malta to find a doctor, because two of them had gunshot wounds, which drew the interest of the sheriff there. So the sheriff got out his wanted posters and figured for sure one of them may have been Kid Curry. You know these gunshot wounds may have come from that shootout you had at that cabin."

"Yeah," I said. "Wow, Kid Curry, huh."

"Yeah, and horse thieving is one of the activities he's wanted for, so it sounds like something he might have done," the sheriff replied.

I looked at Jesse. He shrugged and smiled, saying, "Good shootin' partner."

"But I don't want to shoot anybody," I said. "I just want what is rightfully mine."

They both went on eating as if it were just another day in the wild west.

Between bites, the sheriff said, "Anybody out here who has anything, has had to fight for it."

"Yeah," Jesse said, "you Dakota plow boys will eventually learn there's a whole different set of rules out here."

"Yeah, I know," I said. "Out here possession is ten-tenths of the law if your gun is better than the other guy's. But my Pa came out to western Dakota and settled with a lot of other folks and he has never had to fire a shot to protect any of it."

"Yeah, well the outlaws are being squeezed out here into these bad lands and I'm afraid law and order'll be slow coming. Besides . . .," Jesse said.

"Besides what?" I asked.

"Besides your food is getting cold and you'll need that energy to fight the bad guys."

They both chuckled. I went to eating.

"The new train runs all the way out there now," the sheriff said. "You could load 'em up and be safe."

"We thought about that," Jesse said, "but it's expensive and we need to break them before we get there. They're worth more broke to ride."

"Besides," I said, "I hear those trains get robbed out here too."

"Yeah," the sheriff said, "that's a fact."

We bought another old two dollar saddle in Glasgow, so we had four mustangs weighted down with supplies and rocks.

I suggested we run them hard and tire them out, so they couldn't buck very hard. Jesse agreed. He wanted to get out to that gold country as fast as I did. Besides, that would have us passing between Landusky and Malta in the middle of the night. Jesse never caught on and we rode quickly through that country. Alternately sleeping on the horses, we rode for a day, a night, and the whole next day before we camped. The long hard ride worked. We had broken several of the horses by now.

We were following along the north side of the big river and at times could catch a glimpse of it. One day we got a particularly long view of the river. We noticed a large boat with two smokestacks on it.

"Paddle wheeler," Jesse said. "They bring lots of supplies and people up the river."

"I wonder what will happen now that the trains are bringing supplies?" I asked.

"Yeah," as we enjoyed the sight. "Probably won't be around very long."

The next day it looked like we weren't going to get all the horses broke by the time we got there, so we went to work hard breaking.

Jesse got frustrated with going through the whole bridle break, saddle break, weights, and then tire them out to exhaustion so they couldn't buck so hard. So he decided to try it Indian style. He jumped from the saddle of the horse he had just broke onto a bareback and grabbed the mane. Next thing I saw Jesse flying headfirst over that horse's head. I knew I had to get those horses away to keep them from stomping on him.

I got them split away just in time, but now they were running everywhere, so I tried to get them herded back up a short distance away. I noticed Jesse was not moving. He still laid there in a crumpled mess, not moving a muscle.

I threw one of the oat sacks out on the ground hoping it would bring them back in as I rode over to Jesse. He was breathing but wasn't moving even when I yelled at him. I was getting a little worried. He had a large black and blue knot on his head. There was blood in his hair.

I dragged him over to some rocks and brush, his head hung limp. I got his canteen and laid that wet bandana on the knot. There wasn't much else I could do for him right then, so I figured I needed to secure the horses.

I roped the two that always wanted to wander and tied them. Then I gathered the others around the oats.

I went back to Jesse. He was breathing. His heart was beating, but he was out. I'd heard people had been knocked clean out, to come to later, but I'd never seen it before. I washed his head and face with cold water but no response. I even tried to slap him lightly a couple of times.

Wow, I was in a predicament. I had twenty five horses to wrangle and a hurt man that I didn't know how bad he was. Night was coming on. How would I keep the horses there? They had eaten the oats and were now mingling around.

Did Jesse need a doctor, or would he come out of it? I examined the knot. The bleeding had stopped. I laid the cold wet bandana on it again. His heart was beating. Should I abandon the horses and get him to a doctor? Would he do that for me? Or maybe I shouldn't move him.

Night was coming on and I didn't know how far the next town or ranch was. I mounted up and gathered the horses. They seemed to settle down. Darkness was coming so I decided to stay right here right now. While riding the herd I could think.

The night brought cold, so I got Jesse's bed roll and covered him and made him as comfortable as I could. Still nothing, and nothing I could do, so I may as well go out and ride the herd. I chuckled. I could hear him now, "you let the herd go just because I got a knot on my head?"

Some of those wild horses still wanted to wander so I was busy keeping them in. Later that night the wolves or coyotes started to howl far off. That was actually good because the horses came back in and huddled into the herd. Then I could get a fire going by Jesse and make coffee and something to eat.

I sat there looking at him breathing and wondering how long a man could be out cold like that and survive. I guess I was going to find out.

I went out and walked around the herd. The howling was working. The horses were all there, so I went back over and sat down. Then I thought this would be a bad time for the rustlers to come by. I would be in a fix without Jesse's guns. I guess I'd have to give up the herd to save his life, but I better save our two horses, so we had something to ride.

I saddled up the two and put them behind us and the fire. I sat back down to think some more on my situation. Before I knew it, I was awakening from deep sleep. By the look of the fire, I had slept for several hours. I threw wood on the fire and woke up a little bit, drank some more coffee, and ate some biscuits.

I looked at Jesse, still breathing. He didn't look any different. I got up and walked around the herd. They were settled down good now, even though the howling could barely be heard. I thought I'd saddle up one of the others and ride out and look around.

Next thing I knew I woke up very cold in the saddle. I dismounted and went over to the fire. Before I got a cup of coffee down, I could see twilight barely over the horizon.

Jesse still laid there. Maybe I could make a travois and carry him somewhere. I found two long pieces of wood and made the travois. All the wild horses were too skittish to be trusted to pull it. I decided I'd have to ride the horse with the travois and herd the horses at the same time. This was going to be tricky.

I got Jesse loaded in the travois as easily as I could and headed the horses west. After about five miles the horses got restless again and started wandering. I stopped and tied off and got another horse to round them up. This wasn't going to work. I was really in a fix now. I didn't have enough rope to tether them all together so what could I do? I got them all back to the travois and there sat Jesse holding his head and looking around confused.

"What the hell happened?" he asked to no one in particular.

"Your horse threw you and you landed on your head."

"Where the hell am I?" he asked.

"We're heading to western Montana to sell our wild mustangs."

"Oh yeah," he said, quietly pushing up the canteen and pouring water over his head, as if to wash off the cobwebs.

"You going to be okay?" I asked.

No answer. His brain was trying to put two and two together.

"You were knocked out cold," I said. "I had to carry you on that travois, so we could keep heading west."

He laid back down holding his head.

"Just ride there," I said.

"No," he said. "I'll ride. Give me a minute."

As I gathered the horses again, he got up, untied the travois, and got on the horse. We headed out, but after a while he slumped in the saddle half asleep. Still, we were making progress. By early afternoon he seemed to wake up.

He asked if we had anything to eat. We didn't but could see smoke up along the river and figured it for a town. He drank water all the way there.

It was Fort Benton. We got the horses in the stable corral and went to eat. I asked if there was a doctor around. Only a midwife lady that did some doctoring. She cleaned and bandaged Jesse's head and told him he should take it easy for a few days.

"No," he said. "I've been knocked on the head worse than this many times."

I said, "It wouldn't hurt to lay over here a few days."

"No, let's ride," he said.

She looked at me and I shrugged and said, "Okay."

Physically he seemed okay, but mentally he still seemed a little goofy to me, maybe half drunk would be the best way to explain it.

We were told Great Falls was the next big town, about forty miles. We made it in one ride. Late at night I stabled the horses and got us a good hotel room. I figured it was time for a rest. I went out to inquire about the latest gold activity and if anybody was buying horses. When I got back, Jesse had gotten a haircut, shave, and bath and was now in the saloon drinking whiskey. That's all I needed, a knot on the head and whiskey too. He had two saloon girls he was buying drinks for, telling them the great adventure of driving the horses.

"Have a drink, partner," he said.

"No, go ahead. This better be my night to watch the horses. We don't want to lose them now. We're only one day's ride to the gold strike in Helena. I hear that will be the best place to sell them."

"Okay, suit yourself," one of the girls said, "but you'll miss a good party."

"That's okay," I said. "I'll party when we have the money for these horses in our pockets."

"Okay," he said. "Good idea."

I checked on the horses and went to bed. I checked on the horses a couple more times that night and as I went by the saloons, the partying seemed to go on all night. I guess the gold was still flowing.

I finally fell asleep and woke up to daylight. Jesse wasn't around so I dressed and went to check the horses. All was well.

I ate breakfast. A well-dressed man sat at the table next to me.

He asked what my business was? I told him we had some horses we were going to try to sell to the miners for a little more money than the usual going rate back home.

"Shouldn't be a problem at all," he said.

We talked for over a half hour. He told me all about the mining activity around Helena and other parts of Montana. Then I thought how did he know all this, so I asked his business.

"I have a saloon here in Great Falls, but when the big gold pay started in Helena, I built the biggest saloon there, The King's Palace," he said proudly. "Look me up when you get there. Here's my card. I also own partial interest in one of the mines."

Big Jim Harbow, Entrepreneur, The King's Palace.

"Yes, we got everything a man could want there," he said.

The girl with him winked at me just then.

"Oh, I see," I said.

"What do you plan to do when your horses are sold?" he asked.

Just then Jesse showed up, "Did you say we should stay here another day?" he asked.

"Yeah, we'll be rested by tomorrow," I said.

"Loan me another ten dollars then?" he asked.

"Okay," I said handing him the bill. "But I'm leaving early, and I wouldn't know what to do with all that money by myself from all those horses."

"Oh, I'll be there," he said. "I didn't come all this way to miss that."

He rushed off.

"Your partner I take it?" Jim asked.

"Yeah, he's spending his money before he's making it."

"Well, be sure to look me up. The King's Palace. Ask for Big Jim."

"Will do," I said.

I went to working with our horses at the stable corral. Amazingly, I had some sort of mental hesitation to tackling these particular horses head on. I think it had to do with seeing what happened to Jesse.

Jesse was no slouch. He was as good a horse wrangler as I had ever known. He was young, strong, and tough, but that mustang had bested him and almost seriously injured him.

I now worked with a whole new respect for these horses. Working with wild horses was a whole different deal. But when you broke one of these wild mountain mustangs, you had a hell of a horse. I was excited to show these horses in gold country and see what they would bring.

CHAPTER 33

It was a beautiful ride through the mountains from Great Falls to Helena. We were both in awe. I couldn't help but wonder how they found that gold out here in this big country. I decided I better stay with what I knew, horses.

Jesse agreed, "More than nine miners out of ten went broke prospecting."

Helena's gold wealth was conspicuous, lots of big, fancy houses, lots of big, fancy saloons. The party never ended. Lots of other places to spend your gold wealth. Just when I thought Jesse had regained his senses, I looked at him and he was looking around like a kid in a candy store, with a wild look in his eye.

"Wow, what a place," Jesse said.

"Yeah," I said, "a fool and his money are soon parted."

He didn't pay attention to me but was looking around and trying to decide which place to hit first, but he'd have to wait. He was penniless and owed me ten dollars.

"I guess it's your turn to watch the horses tonight."

"Yeah, I guess," he said.

"I think we should get some rope and tie a Hackamore to each of them so we can show them each separately."

"Yeah, good idea," he said.

"I'm going to find Big Jim," I said.

The King's Palace was easy to find, one of the biggest places there was. Big Jim was also easy to find. He was working the crowd and promoting, a perfect man for the saloon business. He waved me over when he saw me.

"Whiskey or beer?" he asked.

"Until my business is over, I think water."

"Oh, one beer won't hurt," he said.

"You sell your horses yet?" he asked.

"No, we just got here."

"Where you gonna sell 'em?" he asked.

"I don't know. I was hoping you could give me a lead," I said.

"Well, it's not hard to sell horses here," he said. "Hey, let's sell them in the pavilion out back."

"Pavilion?" I asked.

"Yeah, the big arena out back. We have events there like boxing matches and such. Have all your horses there by noon," he said. "We'll have a horse sale."

"That would be great," I said. "But what would something like that cost us?"

"Nothing boy, it's a promotion event. Brings in the business you know. We'll have a bar set up out there, real handy to the action. We've had everything out there, but this will be the first horse sale."

A saloon girl came over and said, "Yeah, this should be fun cowboy. What say we start the party now?"

"Uh . . . . I need to buy some new clothes for the sale tomorrow," I finally stammered.

I was rough looking and needed a shave and bath, so I excused myself and promised to be back. After buying new clothes, a shave, and bath, I went back to the stable.

Jesse asked, "Did you get anything arranged?"

"Yeah," I said. "The sale's about noon tomorrow at the saloon."

"We are going to sell them at the saloon?"

"Well," I said, "they have a big open pavilion out back for things like this," I said.

He smiled and said, "Yeah, I guess that could work. . . . I hope it works. We already owe ten dollars for the stable bill."

"Yeah, I know," I said. "I just bought some clothes; paying gold prices in gold country."

We had Hackamore leads on all the horses as we led them to the center of town and to the pavilion. Strung across the street was a big sign, Big Horse Sale Here Today 1:00.

"Wow," Jesse asked, "how did you manage that?"

"Looks like Big Jim does everything big," I said.

We had a large following as we led the mustangs into the pavilion and tied them to the gate across one side of the pavilion.

The pavilion became packed with people. Gunfire. Jesse and I jumped.

"It's just a shooting demonstration," Mary, the saloon girl said laughing.

"Oh yeah."

We had to stay with the horses. They were jumpy, not being used to being around so many people and loud noises. I told Mary to tell Jim to start the sale.

Jim came out and said, "Okay, there's enough people here to have the sale."

"I'll give you five hundred dollars for this one."

"I'll give you six hundred dollars for this one," came shouts from the crowd.

Jim got up into the boxing ring and held up his hands. Everybody became quiet. He went through his "we're having a horse sale here" speech.

He directed Jesse to bring up the first horse. He brought up a broke one with one of the old saddles and bridles on it. He jumped on and rode him around in front of the people.

Hands were going up even before Jim could call the bids. "Five hundred, six hundred, seven hundred, seven hundred fifty, eight hundred dollars."

This was going to be good, I thought as nine hundred was called. Jesse got the horse to rear up and one thousand dollars was bid.

"Sold!" Jim called.

Jesse jumped off hooting and hollering.

"Round for the horse!" he yelled.

Oh no, I thought, he's going to go crazy.

Jim said, "See, I told you, business."

As the rest of the horses went to one thousand dollars and over Jesse said, "See, I told you partner, we're in the money."

The sale went crazy with bids. I lost count. Jim had some of the girls collecting the money. Jesse saw my concern.

"Don't worry about it," he said. "You ever get this much for horses before, even from the Canadians?"

"No," I said in amazement.

At the end, somebody brought Jesse's saddle horse.

"No," I yelled.

Jesse pulled me aside.

"I'm selling him."

"What are we going to ride home?" I asked.

"Remember that river boat?" he said. "It goes right to Williston, right?"

"Right," I said.

With the newer saddle and bridle on him, Jesse's horse brought $1,200.

"Well, I think we can afford a ticket on the paddle wheeler now."

I had to admit that was awfully good money. I seemed to be in a daze as they brought up my horse.

At one thousand two hundred fifty dollars, Jim called, "Sold!"

Jesse was jumping up and down waving his arms for more beer. The girls took care of us. I was more interested in their accounting of our proceeds. Jim and the girls came over. Jim had a big smile and stuck out his hand to shake.

"Brought in the business, huh," he said, sweeping his hand around.

"Yeah," Jesse said, "great," looking at the money.

Alice had all the numbers written down.

Jesse said, "Forget that, give me my share."

He counted it quick, nearly eleven thousand dollars. I think that was more than Jesse had ever seen before.

"Another round for this house!" he yelled.

I cringed. Alice handed me a bag full of bills and three bags with gold coins in them. She then showed me the paper she had the tally on. I put it in the sack and thanked her and Jim.

Jim said, "I have a safe in my office you could use."

"Thanks," I said. "I think I know where to put this."

I found Jesse and took most of his money and went to the hotel room.

If I figured the value of the gold correctly, some fourteen thousand dollars, nearly one thousand dollars a head. Yeah, I'll ride the riverboat home. I found three hiding places in my room to hide the money. I left some in my pocket. I emptied the cash into my bag and hid it. I put some rocks in the bag, then found Jim, and put the bag in his safe. Enough people saw me so I figured they would all think the money was in his safe.

Jim came and found me, bought me a drink, and said, "The reason I did that is because now that you and Jesse are done with your business, I sure could use you in my employ."

Mary winked at me again. Oh great. I did my best to explain that I had to get back. I would need to help my family on the farm, and I had more horses to take care of.

"Where is Jesse anyway?" I asked.

The girl that had been with him pointed at the back door, which meant the place to get rid of the beer.

"He's been out there for a while," she said.

"Oh great, I better check."

I ran out there and sure enough, two big guys were trying to find out where his money was. I snuck up behind them and swung the leather pouch with the gold coins as hard as I could. The outlaw went down. The other one ran.

I hustled Jesse back to the hotel room. I felt his pockets and he had lost all the money that he had.

The next day we caught one of the many stages that ran between Helena and Great Falls. We purchased our steamboat tickets but had to wait on board until departure early the next morning.

Jesse had rested up by then, and swore off any more partying, so I gave him the rest of his money. But as we heard, the paddle wheeler provided entertainment to pass the time going down the river. I was wondering how long Jesse could hold out before he succumbed to temptation.

It was all there, just like the King's Palace saloon. All sorts of gambling, shows, girls, and more kinds of alcohol than I knew existed. Jesse and I were laying low and just watching the show when Katrina showed up. I whispered to Jesse that I didn't think it was a good idea to let anybody know you have a lot of cash on you.

"I know," he said adamantly. "Believe me I don't intend to."

"A drink for you boys?" she asked.

"Water," I said.

"Me too," Jesse repeated.

She laughed. I put up two bits.

"What's the matter?" she asked. "Aren't you boys up for a good time?"

Then after thinking about it, Jesse put out a dollar. She brought over drinks and a friend, Paulina.

"Come on Bill, isn't this better than wrangling those horses across the badlands dodging bad guys?"

"Yeah, this is addicting," I admitted, 'better than getting bucked off and landing on your head."

The girls laughed and wanted to hear the whole story. Jesse could tell it better than anyone. We were having a good time. I started to notice a lot of tough looking characters hanging around. I didn't like the looks of them at all. I told Jesse we would be in Williston tomorrow and that we needed to get some sleep. He agreed but said he'd stay a little longer.

"Okay," I said, as I excused myself.

"Oh, don't worry about him," Katrina said. "We'll take care of him."

"He needs taking care of," I said. "Don't let him get any more bumps on his head."

They laughed.

Jesse gave me a shove and said, "I can take care of myself. Go to bed."

I had to admit it was good not to have any horses to worry about. They were worth so much money in this country that it seemed like half the people out here were out to steal them. This was luxury. I looked out at those badlands we had crossed just a few days before. I was crossing the same country, but now I had a nice warm bed to sleep in and no worries.

When I hit that bed, I was asleep. I knew I had slept several hours when my door exploded in thunder. Somebody was pounding on it with something. A woman's voice, Katrina.

"You've got to save him. They're going to kill him."

I looked through the little peep hole on the door. Katrina was pounding on it with her shoe. I opened it.

"You've got to come. They robbed him and wanted to get rid of the witness."

Still half asleep I got on most of my clothes before she dragged me out. I was following her when I realized I forgot my gun. Should I go get it?

By then we were on the lower level deck and two men were about to throw Jesse overboard. I knew I couldn't get there in time to catch Jesse, so I ran and hit the two men as hard as I could and all four of us went overboard.

I grabbed Jesse as soon as we hit the water. Luckily for all of us, the paddle wheeler had just gone through an area of reeds and water weeds and was dragging a bunch of it that we grabbed onto. I had Jesse and was hanging onto the reeds. The two outlaws were dragging behind us.

The closest one pulled his gun and tried to fire at us. POOF, the powder was wet. He pulled the trigger several more times, nothing. He held it to try and reload it. I reached back and grabbed it by the barrel and used it as a hammer to pound on him. He got it back and went to reload it. I couldn't move or I would let Jesse go.

I had no gun, but my knife was in my pants pocket, but I still couldn't use it. Then I thought if I cut the reeds off behind me, they and the reeds would be cut loose. I hacked frantically at the reeds. The outlaw saw what I was doing and started hammering at me with his nonfunctioning gun. I stabbed at him and cut some more.

He clawed his way up to me. We fought back and forth with one hand each. He got near me and I kicked him away with both legs. That caused the chunk of reeds he was hanging onto to finally break away and down the river they went.

I tried to pull Jesse back up the reeds to the boat. I was weak and cold from the water. I was just about to give up and try to swim to shore, when the big paddle wheels started to slow, then slowed more until they finally stopped.

Katrina was pointing at us to two crewmen who threw us a round float on a rope. They pulled us up alongside the boat. I tied the rope around Jesse, and they pulled him up. I was too stiff, cold, and weak to pull myself in, so I tied the rope around myself. When I got on deck I couldn't hardly stand. The cold water had revived Jesse. I don't think I had ever been so exhausted in my life. Jesse was sitting up feeling his pockets.

"No money?" I asked him.

From the look on his face, I knew.

Katrina stepped up with a stack of bills in her hand. I started laughing.

"Well Jesse, looks like she saved you a second time."

Jesse had the most astonished look on his face as he looked at the money.

"Where's your gun? Where's your hat?" I asked him.

"I don't know," he said rubbing his head.

"How much does he have left?" I asked Katrina.

"I think about half," she said, "maybe $5,000 to $6,000."

"Easy come, easy go," I said. "I still got all of mine."

Then it struck me, thinking about my money in my room. Had I locked the door when I left in such a hurry? I was running and slipping down the wet deck. Got inside and ran to my door. My heart sank as I tried the door. It was unlocked. I yanked it open, but I knew I was okay because the .30 Winchester was laying on the bed. That would have been the first thing they would have taken, but it was all there.

Thank God it was the middle of the night and nobody was prowling around looking for unlocked doors. We were both tired. We went to bed.

"Don't worry, I'm going to keep this well hidden from now on so nobody can find it," he said, as he walked down the hall with Katrina.

CHAPTER 34

I was sleeping hard when somebody beat on my door.

Katrina said, "Only about an hour to Williston."

I jumped up, got dressed, washed up, and then I was hungry.

Jesse, Katrina, and Paulina waved me over to their table. A big breakfast was served.

"Better than sitting out there on the prairie, chewing on dried meat, and quail eggs, huh," Jesse said.

"Yeah, I couldn't agree more," I said. "It should be though, for what we spent."

"Fifty dollars aint bad for this ride," Jesse said.

"How much did you have in Helena?" I asked.

"You know, over ten thousand dollars."

"Yeah, and now how much you got now?" I asked.

With a red face he said, "Over half."

I laughed and said, "This dumb plow boy's got almost all of mine. Ha ha. Now who can't handle the wild west? I almost have to borrow you a horse to get home," I said.

"I'm not riding," he said.

"Great, you decided to stay and help me train these horses?" I asked.

"No, I'm going to float. We're going to float," he said, looking at Katrina.

"Where you going to float to?" I asked. "You're going the wrong way."

"No, the Platte River runs into the Missouri and the steamers go up the Platte to Wyoming. You could come down the same way this fall. We'll have broken mustangs ready to go up and get the rest of that herd," he said. "Think about that money. Losing five thousand dollars will be chicken feed then."

341

"Yeah, let's do that," I said. "But I think we might flood the horse market."

"Well, then we'll sell the rest in Canada," he said.

"Well, I tell you," I said, "these contraptions are taking over. The steamboats and trains are every-where now."

"Oh, don't worry partner," Jesse stated. "There'll always be a need for good horses."

"I hope you're right, partner."

The boat was docking at Williston. I shook Jesse's hand and said, "Good luck getting home with the rest of your money."

Glancing at Katrina, he punched me lightly on the shoulder and said, "Don't worry about me. You just worry about us rounding up the rest of those wild mustangs."

"You know I wouldn't miss that, all two hundred."

"Two hundred fifty," he replied.

I had to buy an old horse in Williston to get home. I then went to the leather goods shop and bought the best saddle they had. I got a lot of stares and head shakes as I rode out of town with a saddle that was worth three times as much as the horse that it was on.

Seeding had started by the time I got home. We had a draft horse team, an ox team, and two mule teams by now. I wasn't in trouble though because both Bob and Noa had been able to drive a team, but I was relegated to driving a mule team and soon gained a lot of respect for these animals. We seeded over two hundred acres, more than we had ever before - corn, wheat, barley, and oats.

We would need it all. We had over forty horses, cattle, pigs, and mules. We worked hard all summer on the farm and training the horses. Bob, Noa, and I worked with great anticipation of our coming trip south to Shilo Ranch and then up after the mustangs. How many would we get this time? What kind of trouble would we run into?

We would need more hands, especially if we were lucky enough to get more of the wild horses. I thought about asking my brother, Barney, to come, but then thought no because of all the work around here. I was leaving my horses here for them to take care of while we were gone. I was paying a lot of wages to everybody except Noa and Bob, who wanted horses instead of money.

I was still trying to teach them the value of a dollar, but it was a tough sell. Horses were money to the Indians. But I shouldn't complain, they had worked hard for them. Bob took the little gray speckled stallion he had been working with. I asked him and sure enough he dreamed of having his own breeding herd someday. Noa was not so particular.

"That's because he would probably sell it if he ever needed money," Bob said.

I also gave them the old mare for Bob's father to help pull the fish out of the ice.

We worked our mustangs hard that summer in anticipation of our next big try at the wild horses. The Canadians hadn't been down all summer and I couldn't help but wonder if that market was getting weak.

There was a girl, Maryetta. I guess I first met her in church. She came from Norway and was staying with the relatives who had sponsored her. Eventually she came to live at our house, helping my mother with cooking and maintaining the house. My sister was gone and there were six hungry men working. She was nice to have around.

One day she asked me to show her the horses, so I began to tell her all I knew about horses.

She said, "Really, I just wanted to talk, because my English isn't so good you know."

I smiled at her and said, "You sound just like my grandmother from Minnesota. I understand you very well."

"The more I talk, the better my English gets," she said. "How about can you teach me to ride the horses? They are very beautiful."

I would love to teach her to ride, I thought, but then remembered we only had wild, barely trained and broke horses. We were working on them hard, but we didn't have anything gentle enough for a beginning rider. What could I tell her that wouldn't sound like I was putting her off?

So, I asked, "You didn't ride horses in Norway?"

"Horses mostly only pulled wagons there," she said. "We traveled mostly by boat."

"So, you've never been on the back of a horse?"

"No," she said.

How was I going to handle this, I wondered? I decided to show her.

I left her outside the corral, climbed in, and roped a half trained one. I got him into the shoot, got a saddle and bridle on him, kicking and biting all the way. I jumped on him and kicked the shoot open. He came out kicking, jumping, bucking, and biting. I got him spurred into a run. We ran around the pasture and then came back to the yard.

She backed up wide eyed. The horse was trying to bite but I would kick him in the muzzle every time he tried it.

Maryetta said, "Oh, I don't think I can ride such an animal."

Something spontaneous hit me and I scooped her up into the saddle in front of me. We left the front yard at full speed with Maryetta screaming. We rode the horse hard until it was tired enough to walk.

"Wow," she said. "The horses in Norway are nothing like this."

"Yeah, these horses are wild, and it takes a lot of breaking before a beginner can ride them."

She turned, looking at me with a funny smile on her face.

I suddenly got the strangest, oddest urge to grab her and kiss her. Wow, I thought. How inappropriate would that be. I hardly knew this girl. I set her down to get that thought out of my head. I got down and started unsaddling and putting the horse away.

"That was a ride I will never forget in my life," she said, with a big smile on her face.

"I hope you don't," I said. "Horses can be dangerous, but I promise you I'll get one gentle for you someday."

"I would really like that," she said. "Soon I hope."

My heart was pounding. I didn't know if it was from riding the horse or was it because I was close to her. We talked and walked around the farm before going back to the house.

"I'll try to gentle a horse for you," I said, "but I have to leave soon to go south and try and get some more horses."

"I know," she said.

"But it shouldn't take that long," I said.

Was I being too presumptive about her being here? Suddenly, I was confused.

"Okay," she said, without the smile.

I didn't sleep much that night thinking about the day. Sunday came and instead of trying to get out of going to church, I was trying extra hard to look my best for church. I stayed close to Maryetta and talked to her. She seemed to like that. Everybody seemed to stare at us.

After church we had Sunday dinner. After Barney and I took care of the teams, we went to the house to eat. The only place left at the table was next to Maryetta. I looked at my mom and dad. They were smiling at me funny.

Both Bob and Noa noticed that I was working extra hard to gentle one of the older mares.

"We don't have time to more than half break them," Noa said. "We leave soon for the mustangs."

"Yeah, I know," I said.

I surprised myself. My brain had been one hundred percent focused on the next mustang roundup. All of us involved had one question in mind: how many this time? Two hundred? Two hundred plus? That was the ultimate goal. But now I was preoccupied.

The day came. We were packed and goodbyes were said all around. I went over to say goodbye to Maryetta. She had a small, straight-lipped smile on her face. Spontaneously I gave her a quick hug and went and jumped on my horse. We were all waving at each other. I could see what I thought was a bigger smile on her face now. Then we were gone.

I couldn't get my mind off trying to read something into her bigger smile. I overheard Barney and Carl saying something about her moving back to her relatives now that there weren't so many men to feed. Would she leave? I figured my mom still needed the help.

"Come on, you're usually leading, now you're falling behind," Bob yelled.

CHAPTER 35

Our first plan was to ride hard for Miles City. I wanted to find Pem. I loved talking to the old cowboy who came out here before there were any towns. We rode hard and got there in only three days. We bypassed Miles City and went directly to the cantina south of town.

There were only two horses there. We went in. Two cowboys sat to the side. I didn't recognize them as any of Pem's men. We went up to the bar and ordered a drink and food.

"Pemberton been around?" I asked.

"Haven't you heard?" the barkeep said. "Big trouble over there. He never returned and the place got burned off."

"You mean he never showed up from the last time we were here?"

"Right," he said. "Been upwards of a year now."

Wow, I didn't know what to say.

"Any of his men still around?" I asked.

"Couple of them in here the other day, but I think they were planning on leaving. Going back to Texas I think."

I thought this over as I ate. I decided to go over to his place to see what was there. One end of the house was burned off and some of the outbuildings were gone. Rifles poked out of the windows as we rode up.

"Pem, you in there?" I yelled.

"No, he's gone," a Mexican voice came back.

"I'm Bill. I've been here before talking to him about horses."

A head popped up in the burned-out hole in the wall. He looked at us and smiled.

"Oh, I remember you. You go after horses."

"Yes," I said. "What happened?"

He turned around and came out through the door.

"Pem go to Texas and visit his people and come back with some stock. But he doesn't come back for over a year. We know something happened to him."

"Wow," I said. "What did the sheriff do?"

"We no talk to him. One of the men see Pem's horse in town. He told the sheriff and then the fire came." He pointed at the burned buildings.

"What happened to the stock?" I asked.

"All gone except what we have here."

We walked up to the house. The three Mexicans looked bewildered.

"What about the other men?" I asked.

"All go to work for the big outfits," he said. "We want to go back to Texas, but we don't have enough money."

"What are you going to do?" I asked.

"I don't know. Work for somebody until we have enough money."

I thought about it and said, "Do you want to work for me?"

"Yes," the man called Manuel said. "Better to work for you than anybody around here."

"Can we stay here tonight?" I asked.

"Yes, there is room," he said.

"Okay. Bob and Noa, you stay here. I'm going into town and talk to the sheriff," I said.

It was late in the day, but the sheriff was there. I went in and he remembered me. So, I asked if those outlaws ever showed up for their guns.

"No," he said, laughing.

"Well, I came to ask about Pemberton."

"Oh yes, I know all about Pem," he said.

"What do you think happened?" I asked.

"Either an accident or foul play," the sheriff said. "And then the vultures moved in."

"Yeah, that's about how I figured it too," I said.

"The cowboy riding what the Mexican claimed was Pem's horse said he was mistaken. The horse was branded over, so I had no proof of anything."

"No body found anywhere?" I asked.

"No."

"Was the cowboy from one of the big outfits around here?" I asked.

"Yes," he said, "one of the biggest."

"That figures," I said. "With no body there's no crime."

"Pem could be walking around somewhere in Texas right now for all we know."

"Yeah," I said, "but I doubt it."

"Yeah, I know. I doubt it, too," the sheriff replied.

I looked at him. He looked at me with a slight shrug to his shoulders.

I said, "If I was to go snooping around..."

I didn't get finished before he said, "Don't do it. You might end up like Pem."

"So, the wild west is as wild as ever," I said.

"Oh yeah," he returned. "We've had eight or ten cases like that over the years, unsolved, but we keep our ear to the ground just in case."

"Okay, great, sheriff. I'll check in with you on my return trip."

A shiver went up my spine as I rode back. We came through here with horses and must have been lucky not to have been bothered. I got back with supplies and told them we were out of here early in the morning.

Manuel, Hector, and Eduardo had seven horses, five cows, a pig, and a wagon. So, we would be traveling slower now. But there didn't appear to be any snow in the mountains yet, so we were early anyway.

I had a bad, eerie feeling. Maybe it was the probable murder of Pemberton. We would probably never know what happened to him.

I was also in a rush. I wanted to get down there, get the horses, and get back. I really didn't know why. Was it Maryetta? I didn't think so, but something was making me subconsciously antsy to get back.

Last year we were foot-loose and without a worry, out on a great adventure. But this year was different. After last year, I was now very aware of all the dangers. I should have felt better. There were six of us now. We were all armed. The Mexicans all had guns. Not very good guns, but they were armed, which was worth something.

The wagon broke down a couple of times, which added to my anxiety. We had to stay in a small town one day to get all the wheels fixed. There still was no visible snow in the mountains. Would we be stuck there waiting for snow?

All these things were bouncing around in my head. I didn't sleep much those days with everything that was going on.

With no snow we moved right along. Then one day, there, just around the bend was the Shilo Ranch. I didn't know what to expect, but there was Slim working. He saw us coming and yelled at the house. Jesse came out, big smile, looking happy.

He handed me a bottle of whiskey and said, "You look like you need to wash the trail dust off."

Wow, was he right. For some reason that drink seemed to wash all my anxiety away.

"Great, you brought extra wranglers."

"Yeah," I said, making introductions all around.

Then I saw the reason for all the cheery attitude. Katrina and Paulina came walking out of the house. They laughed when they saw the look on my face.

"Bet you didn't think you'd see us here, huh."

"Boy, you can say that again," I said.

"Well partner, two hundred head," Jesse yelled.

"I'm here," I said, taking another drink of the whiskey.

Jesse pointed at Noa who was looking at that bottle. I handed it to him.

We brought a couple of bottles on the trail. They disappeared somehow, but Noa had always held up his end.

"About time," Jesse said.

"Yeah," I said, "but no snow yet."

"One of these first days," he said.

The party atmosphere took over. Everybody's dreaming of two hundred plus horses at one thousand dollars apiece. A big dream, I thought.

I threw myself into working with the horses and other ranch work, anything to keep my mind occupied. Two days later, snow fell in the mountains. Not much, but the mountains were white. Everybody was getting ready for an early morning departure.

Morning dawned to a clear blue sky. We were all excited and riding hard. We got to the ridge near sundown.

"Horses are there," Noa said.

Jesse said, "We're going to have to work fast."

He and I led our horses to look over the ridge to see if the horses were there. We walked to the edge of the trees and there they were. Horses were strung up and down the valley for as far as we could see. Jesse and I stood there looking dumbstruck. They were there.

I was trying to spot the big gray speckled stallion when Jesse said, "What are we waiting for?"

Just then our two mountain mustangs began neighing and whickering very loudly and in the blink of an eye, all those horses disappeared up the valley and out of sight.

Jesse and I looked at each other like, I thought you were a horse expert. Laughter erupted behind us.

Laughing hysterically, Noa said, "And you didn't think horses could talk."

"What did he say?" Jesse asked me.

"You don't want to know," I said.

"Well, it wasn't that damn funny," Jesse said.

"Yeah, I agree," I said. Damn, outsmarted by horses again.

Bewildered, we decided to go elk hunting. We went to the next mountain over so the shooting wouldn't spook the mustangs. But by late the next day, it clouded up and late that night the snow came. Just before sunup, the snow was falling heavily.

Noa said to me, "I think the mustangs are back."

"In the valley?" I asked.

"Yes, they are there," he said.

Smiling skeptically, I asked, "Did you ride over there and see them?"

"No," he said pointing up, "the snow will bring them."

We had the fire and coffee going and by now Jesse was the only one still sleeping. I went over and woke him up.

"Noa thinks the horses are back in the valley," I said.

Rubbing his sleepy head, Jesse asked, "Did Noa ride over there and see them?"

"No," I said. "He thinks the snow brought them back down."

"Oh, 'he thinks'," Jesse said. "We were on the trail of some big elk last night and we should jump them today."

"Well," I said, "Noa has the best horse sense of any man I've ever known."

Jesse got up, got a coffee, and looked at the snow and said, "Well, let's go see how much horse sense he's got."

I knew the horses would take Jesse's mind off the elk.

As we were riding back to the ridge Jesse said, "This time we'll leave these damn horses back down the hill."

"Damn expensive horses," I corrected him.

"Yeah," he said.

Noa, Jesse, and I walked through the trees to the top of the ridge. The snow was falling so heavily now that we couldn't see much. Noa put his finger to his lips. It was dead silence, but I thought I could hear something. So did Jesse. I thought I could glimpse a ghostly outline of a horse through the falling snow. Jesse motioned us back.

Noa said, "Yes, they are there. I think I can sneak out and get a better look."

Jesse and I looked at each other.

"Oh hell," Jesse said, "what have we got to lose? Let's try it."

I agreed, "Let's go."

We made a plan. I would lead, then Bob and Noa. Jesse would be next with the Mexicans following with their slower horses.

"Whenever you're ready," Jesse said.

With my hand over my horse's muzzle, I kicked her hard. We exploded over the ridge into the murky snow fall. There they were, looking up at the noisy intruders. I curved left to encompass as many of the wild horses as I could. Our surprise was perfect.

I had to guess where the rock walls were on the other side of the canyon. My guess must have been close because the echoes started and the horses that were in the valley shied down. This was my first ride on a mustang in high country and her big lungs showed. We crossed that valley in no time and almost ran into the rock wall on the other side. We turned, ran, jumped, shooting, and yelling to keep the horses headed downhill. I couldn't see if we had five hundred or five. It was too snowy.

I yelled at Bob, "It don't matter. We'll take what we got. Keep shooting."

We had them moving down pretty good now. By the time we were all busy reloading, we reached an area of less snowfall and the horses stopped and mingled. Then, just like before, a big stallion came out to challenge their antagonizers. But then another one came out. They looked like they were ready to bolt between us and the whole herd would probably follow. Jesse saw it too and was taking aim.

I spurred my horse, a mare who was reluctant to ride at the stallions. I spurred her hard and ran between them. They turned to face me, but I rode through and they ended up facing each other. One and then the other started pawing and before we knew it, the fight was on, hooves, teeth, and then blood. Wow, I would never have guessed the savagery of these animals.

"Shoot!" I yelled.

I tried to shoot one in the rear to sting him and take his mind off the fight. One took after the other and I was in the middle of it.

I decided to shoot one of them, but my horse got bit in the rear and went to bucking. I was hanging onto my rifle and not the horse, and off I went. I was now in the middle of it on foot in a cloud of snow. Then a loud shot rang out and the action stopped. The big aggressor just stood there.

Noa chased the other battered stallion back down into the herd and began firing, then everybody did, and the herd slowly began herding back down the valley. Bob rounded up my horse and brought it to me. We kept the horses headed down.

The last I saw of that big stallion, he was still standing there, not moving as he disappeared into the snowfall. Jesse looked at me and shrugged. I gave him a thumbs up. We followed what we had done before. Bob went down and cut the herd up over the low ridge into the valley that led down to the Shilo corrals.

"We got 'em!" Jesse yelled.

"Yeah, but I don't think there's two hundred."

"There's more than we got last year," he said.

"Yeah, I think so," I said, "Noa will know."

"Okay," he said. "We listen to Noa from now on. I just wish I could understand him."

CHAPTER 36

Slim was checking out the new horses when we got to the ranch.

"I wish I could have been with you."

"Well, there's a lot of winter left. We could see if we could get some more," Jesse said.

"I think I got enough," I said. "I gotta get back."

"You getting old on us partner?"

"No," I said. "I just got things going on."

"Okay," he said. "There's always next year."

"Yeah," I said.

Noa came in and said, "More than seventy, but less than eighty."

"Better than nothing," I said.

Then Noa told Slim about our horses neighing and scaring all the horses away. They both laughed hysterically.

"Was it that funny?" I asked.

"I didn't think so," Jesse said.

Noa and Bob were already sorting out the docile ones they thought they could break easily.

"I want to go in a couple days," I told them.

"Okay boss."

Jesse and Slim decided to send most of their half with us. The chance of getting upwards of one thousand dollars apiece was too tempting. We broke five before we left.

Upon reaching the central flat area of Wyoming, we saw two large cattle herds headed north. We passed one and were soon herding beside the second.

A rider came over and before I recognized him, he said, "I figured it was the Montana kid."

It was Harlen.

"I knew it had to be you running that many horses through outlaw country," he said.

"Oh, don't worry about the outlaws, we shot them all," I said laughing.

Jesse rode up and I introduced him. We talked for over an hour.

"Well, you can trail along with us if you want," he said.

"I'd like to but we're pushing these wild ones, keeps them together. When we slow down, they tend to wander. Where you holden up there now?" I asked.

"Well, don't rightly know," he said. "We'll have to herd around until we find an open spot."

"Maybe I'll see you around up there," I said.

"Okay."

"The Montana kid," Jesse said, pointing at me.

"Yeah, next thing I know is some penny dreadful writer will come looking for me."

We both laughed. We went by Rocky Point, the place where the last incident had started.

Whenever we saw Indians or riders, we would put all seven riders on that side of the herd, so they would figure there was an equal number of riders on the other side. So, seven armed men became fourteen or fifteen. It worked. Nobody bothered us. We skirted around Miles City at night. The river was still frozen by Williston, so we made it across the ice okay. We stayed there the night.

I left early the next morning with a string of five horses. I rode them hard all the way home. Barney, Dad, and Carl came out to see the new horses.

"Is that all you got?" Carl asked.

"No," I said. "They're bringing up the rest. We need to sort out these corrals so we can fit sixty horses in them."

"It'll be a tight fit," Dad said.

"Well, we'll be taking almost half of them to western Montana in a few days."

Nobody said anything about Maryetta. My mother came out and said she had hot food.

"I'm hungry," I said. "Let's go eat."

As I walked through the door, I was telling Mom that six more hungry cowboys were coming, and they would need lots of . . . There she was, wearing an apron and working at the stove.

"Did you catch any more?" she asked.

"Lots," I said. "You stayed."

"I just got back," she said. "We knew there would be more to feed."

"Oh yeah," I said. "Good."

I couldn't think of anything to say.

"Do you need any help?" I asked.

"Well, if you're not too busy, we always need water," she said.

I ran out with two buckets and came back. My mom smiled at me and went by. Maryetta was there and looked better than I ever thought. She brought the food.

I said, "Why don't you sit down."

She did.

"No gentle ones this time?" she asked.

"No, wilder than ever," I said.

The rest of the horses arrived so I went out to help corral them. We all came in to eat. I introduced Jesse and they stared at each other for a while.

"When are we heading for Helena?" I asked.

"Day after tomorrow," he said.

Then Noa told the story of our horses talking to the wild ones to make them all run away. Nobody could understand him, but his hand gestures and facial expressions were funny. Bob filled in the blanks and everybody was laughing.

Jesse asked, "Was it really that funny?"

I started laughing, too, and said, "Yeah, I guess it was."

The next morning I was showing Maryetta the new horses.

"You make a lot of money with them."

"Well, I have, yes. But the markets might be getting weak."

"You'll go soon to western Montana?" she asked.

"Yes, I don't know if I want to though."

"You must if you want the good money."

"Yes, of course. You're right," I said. "What are you going to do?"

"I don't know yet," she said. "Why do you ask?"

My heart was pounding, but I had to ask, "Mary, are you going to be here when I get back?"

"Do you want me to be here when you get back?" she smiled.

I said, "Yes, I think I would."

"Okay," she said, and we hugged.

We held hands and walked, looking at the horses.

"You really like the horses, don't you?"

"Yes," I said. "Having a horse ranch is the only thing I've ever wanted to do."

"This is rugged country out here," she said, "but you are good at it and the horses make good money."

"Well, they have," I said, "but in this rough country nothing is ever guaranteed. Mary, I promise I will make this a fast trip."

"Promise me this," she said. "Make it safer than fast. I have heard the stories."

"Oh, it'll be okay. The outlaws are almost gone, and we have more men this time."

"Good," she said. "I hope so."

I yelled at Bob and Noa, "Day after tomorrow we go."

"Okay."

I tried to find the mares without foals so I could take them out and sell them.

We were herding thirty seven horses when we left. Jesse had twenty, I had twelve, and the Mexicans had five. Bob and Noa stayed to work the horses while I was gone. We pushed hard again, riding half asleep in the saddle at night.

"Now I know your rush," Jesse said.

"Yeah, I thought I had my horse ranching plans all figured out," I said. "Then a woman appears out of nowhere."

"That's usually how it happens," Jesse said. "And the complications begin. A nice house, running water, and getting supplies every other day."

"I guess you have to get one sooner or later," I said. "How's Katrina working out?"

"Great," he said. "She and Paulina are from Russia and came here looking for a better life."

"I hope they find it," I said.

We made it to Helena in record time. Big Jim was gone to the Klondike, the new gold rush in Canada.

"How far is that?" I asked. "And do they need horses up there?"

374

"Don't know," he said. "I just know there aint much going on around here."

We were able to sell half our horses. Jesse took what he could and ended up with four thousand dollars.

"Wow, you were right last year. I should a kept better track of my money. I just didn't realize things could have changed so fast."

"Yeah," I said. "Who knew?"

I had the sense that Jesse had matured with this experience, mentally anyways. They decided to head south from there back to Wyoming and Texas.

When they were out of sight, I bought a ticket for me and my remaining horses on the next train. I had a lot to think about on the way home.

My life, once set as a horse rancher and breeder over in Montana by the spring was now changing. A couple of years ago I could think of nothing else and was always living for the day I could get away and get after those wild horses. Now, I seemed to be thinking about home more than the wild horses. Could Maryetta be the reason for that?

I seemed to have her on my mind all the time. I had seen men change their demeanor when they got involved with a woman. With both the gold field and Canadian horse markets drying up and Mary coming into my life, was I headed for a big change?

My heart was torn. I couldn't help but remember riding wildly fast across that valley herding horses with guns, feeling elation, euphoria, and being on top of the world. I wanted it to never end. I thought I had found my life's work. Slim said it had something to do with the altitude and lack of oxygen somehow.

Could a man go hunting wild mustangs and be married at the same time? Wow, married. I had to think about this, but every time I did, Mary's picture popped into my head, standing there smiling with the apron on, working. But then I thought maybe the horse markets would come back and Mary would take up with somebody else, maybe one of my brothers. They were more stable and around all the time. I had been gone more than home.

Well, I thought, it was up to her. Maybe there was no deciding for me. I guess fate will intervene no matter what I do, just like the horse markets.

CHAPTER 37

She was there and when I got her alone, we hugged.

"Miss me?" I asked.

"A little bit," she said teasing. "Did you miss me?"

"No," I said, "not really. . . because you were on my mind most of the time."

She smiled and said, "So the horse trading didn't go so good."

"No," I said, "Seems the gold fields have dried up and the Canadians are breeding up their own horses by now. But I think there'll be money to be made, just not as much."

I looked at her and asked, "Do you think it's a worthy occupation?"

"Yes," she said. "I can see it's your dream."

"Can it be your dream too?" I asked.

"Well, if you don't mind a girl with not such good English," she said.

"It's good enough for me," I said. "Besides, I've only got a shack over there in Montana."

"Good enough for me," she said. "It can be our dream."

The mares were starting to foal that spring. Noa, Bob, and I were busy because the calves were coming too. My quick calculation, figured with forty horses, I would have something over seventy horses if everything went well. Seventy horses were too many for us to handle. We'd be okay as long as the grass was green, but I had to do something. So I told everybody I needed to go to Canada and find Sem and Arvine. My dad agreed.

Before seeding, I rode north. I'd never been very far up there before. I ended up one hundred miles north by a town they called Regina. I finally found someone who knew Sem, but not Arvine.

"They were wrangling horses up to the Klondike," he said.

"Yeah, the new gold strike?" I asked.

"Yup, as many as they can find," he said.

I left him a message to tell him Bill, south of the border, had horses and to come down.

"Okay," he said.

I returned and we sorted out twenty five of the best and went to breaking the rest hopefully for sale to the Canadians.

Early midsummer, Sem showed up with another wrangler, Merea, and another well dressed man, Oneilly. After the introductions I asked where Arvine was?

"He didn't make it," Sem said. "After we were here, two rustlers came into our camp for the horses. They didn't get anything, but Arvine got a bullet in the back. We tried to get him to see a doctor, but he wouldn't go. After three days, he fell right out of his saddle, dead. We buried him right there."

Shocked, I asked, "How far away were you?"

"Oh, not less than twenty miles north of the border," he said.

"Wow, that was close, the closest we've heard of rustlers around here. Sorry to hear it," I said.

Sem looked at me, shrugged and said, "Luck of the draw, keep your powder dry".

We showed the horses, and they were impressed with their looks, but said the market was at two hundred to three hundred dollars a head right now, maybe more if the horses were broke.

I started telling them about the wild mountain mustangs and how they lived in the mountains.

"Perfect for the north, cold country. They could dig in the snow to forage. Good breeding stock too. There are some stallions in there too."

I could tell Oneilly was interested. I figured him to be the money man. This would be a big sale. He suggested we move them up to the roundup point just south of Regina. We had them ready to go the next morning, nearly seventy head counting all the colts. Bob and Noa went with us. We needed all six of us to wrangle that many up there.

I had the Canadians ride the mustangs on the way up, so by the time we got there, they were sold on the quality of the horses. The roundup point was a sales ring for horses going up to the Klondike.

One last good sale, I hoped, before all the gold strikes dried up. The big rugged muscular horses sold better than anyone expected. I think everybody knew by now how much horses were worth at the gold fields.

I was lucky there were not many other horses at the sale, and I did extremely well. They were getting my money together. Many of the wranglers tried to hire us to help wrangle the horses up to the Klondike. We couldn't do it. We had to go back through the same area that Arvine got shot.

When they brought U.S. greenbacks, I told Bob and Noa we would be riding the night. Anybody seen us taking horses north would know we would be returning with money. I told Bob and Noa to get their rifles out and we would carry them across our saddles so anybody could see them. We rode straight through the night. At early morning we crossed the U.S.-Canadian border unscathed.

I was relieved. I had over thirty five thousand dollars in U.S. currency in my pockets. I told Bob and Noa to head to the farm and get some rest. The bank was just opening when I pulled up.

On my way home I couldn't help but wonder if this was my last great hurrah. The horse markets, the outlaw situation, and, of course, having a family . . . I woke up in the saddle just passing into the farmyard.

I slept all day and night.

That morning I announced, "I hoped I slept in the saddle for the last time."

"Yeah, besides," Carl said, "I think you are getting a little bow legged."

The laughter broke out. I shook my fist at Carl and said, "You are going to do more horse work. Ha ha."

Mary and I were married the next spring. I stayed home all winter. If everything went right, I should have upwards of twenty foals coming.

CHAPTER 38

I built onto the shack in Montana. Bob, Noa, and I were busy fencing and putting in crops. I started a cattle herd. The big gold strikes were over. We were able to sell horses, but at a smaller price.

The quarter horses had not adapted to the northern cold climate as well as the mustangs had, so I bred the best of both herds together. With Bob and Noa's help, we had some of the finest horses around. We were able to sell them for an acceptable price.

The years went by. We had two girls and then two more. Not until the fifth one did I get a boy, Christopher. Mary was proud. The girls were a great help around the ranch.

Homesteading finally came in and Mary had to do the Homestead as I had already Homesteaded in Dakota. That brought lots of neighbors. Settlers came from everywhere for the free land. Small towns started up.

Bob and Noa worked for me when they weren't back with their people. Bob built his herd up to five well-bred, well-trained horses. Soon he was busy with his own herd, so I would send ten or so horses down every year for him and Noa to train. But the trains and a new thing called the automobile were taking over. Individual people could have their own horseless carriage, so the horse market slowed every year. Soon we hardly sold any horses.

I had switched to cattle as my main income source but still maintained a forty to fifty horse herd. With the lack of sales, my herd eventually grew to eighty plus animals. People were starting to talk.

"What's Bill going to do with all those horses?"

Mary would say, "They're our pets."

I would sell one here or there but for not much money. I was beginning to wonder what I would do with them, but then the big war came. Most of Europe was at war and eventually the United States was drawn into it. Our farm income went up, but I still couldn't sell many horses.

The war finally came to an end. Europe was dev-astated. Almost all the animals were killed besides all the people that died. One day we received word that the government was going to be in town to buy horses. The European countries would need all the horses they could get to restart their farming opera-tions as most of the people there were starving.

Two of my neighbors and I put together a herd to take to town the day of the sale. I put in forty five head hoping to sell most of them. Chris was eight years old and could drive the wagon. So, we drove the horse herd and our families followed in the wagons.

It was a festive atmosphere in town. People had great expectation of getting money for livestock they hadn't been able to sell for a while.

The word came back that they were paying one hundred to two hundred dollars a head. Nothing like the good old days, I thought, but I would take it. It had been too long a dry spell and I needed the money with my growing family. As mine went through, I got closer to two hundred than one hundred dollars and was happy. The buyer noticed the hybrid mix of quarter horses and mustangs and asked if I had any more? Well, yes, I did. He offered me two hundred dollars apiece on the spot knowing I had kept the best back for myself.

I had twelve of the best down at Bob's, so I said, "Okay."

"How about your team and saddle horse?"

"Oh, I can't sell them. I wouldn't even be able to get home."

"Yeah, we can," Chris yelled, pointing up the street. "We can get a Model T."

'Yeah," the buyer said. "Four hundred dollars apiece for the three with the saddle."

"Yeah Pa, everybody's getting a Model T. We need one."

"Five hundred dollars," he said. "Last offer."

I didn't think I'd ever see these prices again. I looked at Mary, smiling her approval.

"Hurry Pa, they're going to sell them all."

"Okay," I said, and I was horseless for only the third time in my adult life. I felt worthless or useless or something. I sure hope Bob doesn't sell my twelve down there.

Mary and the girls took a chunk out of the cash pile and Chris led me up to the automobile garage. There I stood with my cash in my hand looking at that contraption. Was I really going to buy one of these Model Ts that was replacing the horse? I felt guilty or strange somehow. Horses, I thought, were the only thing I would ever need, but here I was.

The salesman yelled, "the last one!"

I shoved my money in my pocket. Don't ever let anybody see your money.

"How much?" Chris asked.

"Six hundred dollars."

"Heck Dad, you got that much for one horse."

"Shhh son."

I needed to talk to that boy later, I thought.

"Well, how does it work?" I asked.

"Jump in," he said. "We'll take it for a test drive."

It had a steering wheel and a whole bunch of levers and peddles. He and Christopher told me just how to adjust the levers and hold my foot on the brake pedal. He cranked a handle at the front, and it came to life.

"The engine was running," he said.

He jumped in the other seat and with Chris in the back, he told me to step on a peddle and away we went.

"Don't forget to steer," he said.

"Yeah, watch out for that buggy," Chris yelled.

I finally got it headed down the middle of the road.

"It'll just take some getting used to," the sales-man said.

"Yeah, you don't have to steer a horse."

We got out on the main road and he told me to push the lever ahead. We took off like a shot. My hat flew off and I was steering like crazy. A team came up from the side street and reared and almost turned the wagon over.

"How do we slow down?" I yelled.

"Pull the lever, Pa."

I finally got slowed down and under control.

We passed the women on the street and Chris yelled, "Our new car!"

They waved enthusiastically.

Wow, we went back to the garage.

"We can all fit in here and it has a fold up top, see Pa, for when it rains."

That was nice.

"Pa, it can go faster than the horses and you don't have to feed it every day."

We didn't have a way to get home. Some other people came by and started looking at it.

"Hurry Pa," Chris looked at me.

Just as the girls came up, all excited, I dug out my money.

After the paperwork and the salesman telling us about the gas, oil, and water, we were ready to go. Everybody was already in with all their new bought goods. The salesman turned the crank and away we went.

"Pa, don't go home yet. We want to ride around town."

Drive around town, I never heard of such a thing. They were laughing and waving at all their friends.

Then somebody yelled, "Hey Bill, I never thought I'd see you in one of those things."

"Yeah, me neither," I waved back.

We finally headed home.

"See Pa, even low gear is faster than the horses. Let's try high gear," Chris said.

"It'll go faster?" one of the girls asked.

"Yeah," Chris said, pushing the lever forward.

I grabbed my hat before we took off. The girls were laughing and having fun. I was steering. They seemed to enjoy bouncing over the bumps in the road. I looked at Mary.

She said, "You know Bill, there's no dust coming up from the horses' hooves."

Every time I complained about having to steer, Chris offered to take over. Boy, I wasn't going to win any arguments here, I thought.

To my surprise we got home in about an hour and it was still daylight. We would have been dragging in late at night with the horses, but I kept my poker face. The next morning, I felt funny somehow, knowing I didn't have a horse on my place. I wondered when Bob would bring back my horses. I felt lonesome somehow. I hope Bob didn't sell those horses.

I told Chris, "First chance we get, we're going down to Bob's and get the horses back."

"Okay, Pa. I'll drive her back while you ride."

Mary smiled at me. Nobody complained about having to go to church. They all wanted to show off our new Model T, but by then half the people there had Model Ts. They loved it anyway.

Then somebody joked, "If Bill's got a Model T, that's the end of the horse."

"No," I said. "I'm going down to Bob's and get my horses back."

The conversation from there went to how nice it was to have a Model T.

That afternoon after dinner Chris came running into the house, yelling that the cows were out in the barley field. I panicked. With no horses, I imagined myself out there on foot chasing those cows.

"The Model T," Chris pointed. He was in the seat with everything set.

"Crank," he yelled.

I turned the handle and it started. I got in the driver's seat. Chris and I were after the cows in the Model T. It did well and before long we had the cows headed back. Then Chris hit the horn and the rodeo started. Cows were everywhere. I needed to talk to that boy later, especially about the finer points of horsemanship. Without the horn this time we got all but one back in the pasture. I cut right past him then left to cut him off between the fence and the Model T.

"Faster Pa, he's going to get by us."

I did and we got him, but now the fence was coming up too fast, too fast to turn. I tried to hit the brake. We went through the fence, over the rock pile and ended up in the gully with a flat tire.

"You pull back for the brake," Chris said. "You pushed forward for high gear! . . ."

Oh boy, this never happened on a horse! ! ! !